WE'L

One of the greatest writers of science fiction and fantasy in the world today, Ray Bradbury was born in Waukegan, Illinois, in 1920. He moved with his family to Los Angeles in 1934. He has published some 500 short stories, novels, lays, scripts and poems since his first story appeared in *Weird Tales* when he was twenty years old. Ray Bradbury ives in Los Angeles.

By Ray Bradbury

RAY BRADBURY

We'll Always Have Paris

HARPER
Voyager

Harper Voyager
An imprint of HarperCollins*Publishers*
77–85 Fulharn Palace Road,
Hammersmith, London W6 8JB

www.harpercollins.co.uk

A paperback original 2009
1

A catalogue record for this book is
available from the British Library

ISBN-13: 978 0 00 730364 9

This novel is entirely a work of fiction.
The names, characters and incidents portrayed in it are
the work of the author's imagination. Any resemblance to
actual persons, living or dead, events or localities is
entirely coincidental.

Set in Meridien by Palimpsest Book Production Limited,
Grangemouth, Stirlingshire

Printed in Great Britain by
Clays Ltd, St Ives plc

Mixed Sources

Product group from well-managed
forests and other controlled sources
www.fsc.org Cert no. SW-COC-1806
© 1996 Forest Stewardship Council

FSC

FSC
to promote the respon
Produ
to assure c

Find

BIRMINGHAM LIBRARIES	
HJ	15-Jul-2009
AF	£7.99

With love to my lifetime friend,
Donald Harkins,
who is buried in Paris

Contents

Introduction:
Watching and Writing

The stories in this collection were created by two people: The me who watches and the me who writes.

Both of these creatures inside myself have lived under one sign, which has hung over my typewriter for seventy years: *Don't think, do.*

I haven't thought about any of these stories; they are explosions or impulses. Sometimes they are big explosions of ideas that cannot be resisted, sometimes small impulses coaxed to grow.

My favorite here is 'Massinello Pietro' because it happened to me many years ago, when I was in my early twenties and lived in and out of a tenement in downtown L.A. Massinello Pietro became a friend of mine whom I tried to protect from the police and help when he was brought into court. The short story that was inspired by this friendship is, in many ways, basically true and I simply had to write it.

The other stories, one by one, came to me throughout my life – from a very young age through my middle and later years. Every one of them has been a passion. Every story here was written because I had to write it. Writing stories is like breathing for me. I *watch:* I get an idea, fall in love with it, and try not to think too much about it. I then *write:* I let the story pour forth onto the paper as soon as possible.

So here you are with the works of the two people living inside my skin. Some may surprise you. And that is good. Many of them surprised me when they came to me and asked to be born. I hope you enjoy them. Don't think about them too much. Just try to love them as I love them.

Be my guest.

Ray Bradbury
AUGUST 2008

Massinello Pietro

He fed the canaries and the geese and the dogs and the cats. Then he cranked up the rusty phonograph and sang to the hissing 'Tales from the Vienna Woods':

> *Life goes up, life goes down,*
> *But please smile, do not sigh, do not frown!*

Dancing, he heard the car stop before his little shop. He saw the man in the gray hat glance up and down the storefront and knew the man was reading the sign which in large, uneven blue letters declared THE MANGER. EVERYTHING FREE! LOVE AND CHARITY FOR ALL!

The man stepped halfway through the open door and stopped. 'Mr Massinello Pietro?'

Pietro nodded vigorously, smiling. 'Come in. Do you

want to arrest me? Do you want to throw me in jail?'

The man read from his notes. 'Better known as Alfred Flonn?' He eyed the silver bells on Pietro's shirtsleeves.

'That's me!' Pietro's eye flashed.

The man was uncomfortable. He looked around a room crammed full of rustling birdcages and packing crates. Geese rushed in through the back door, stared at him angrily, and rushed back out. Four parrots blinked lazily on their high perches. Two Indian lovebirds cooed softly. Three dachshunds capered around Pietro's feet, waiting for him to put down just one hand to pet them. On one shoulder he carried a banana-beaked mynah bird, on the other a zebra finch.

'Sit down!' sang Pietro. 'I was just having a little music; that's the way to start the day!' He cranked the portable phonograph swiftly and reset the needle.

'I know, I know.' The man laughed, trying to be tolerant. 'My name's Tiffany, from the D.A.'s office. We got a lot of complaints.' He waved around the cluttered shop. 'Public health. All these ducks, raccoons, white mice. Wrong zone, wrong neighborhood. You'll have to clean it up.'

'Six people have told me that.' Pietro counted them proudly on his fingers. 'Two judges, three policemen, and the district attorney himself!'

'You were warned a month ago you had thirty days to stop this nuisance or go to jail,' said Tiffany, over the music. 'We've been patient.'

'I,' said Pietro, 'have been the patient one. I have waited for the world to stop being silly. I have waited for it to stop wars. I have waited for politicians to be honest. I have waited – *la la la* – for real estate men to be good citizens. But while I wait, I dance!' He demonstrated.

'But *look* at this place!' protested Tiffany.

'Isn't it wonderful? Do you see my shrine for the Virgin Mary?' Pietro pointed. 'And here, on the wall, a framed letter from the archbishop's secretary himself, saying what good I've done for the poor! Once, I was rich, I had property, a hotel. A man took it all away, my wife with it, oh, twenty years ago. Do you know what I did? I invested what little I had left in dogs, geese, mice, parrots, who do not change their minds, who are always friends forever and forever. I bought my phonograph, which never is sad, which never stops singing!'

'That's another thing,' said Tiffany, wincing. 'The neighborhood says at four in the morning, um, you and the phonograph . . .'

'Music is better than soap and water!'

Tiffany shut his eyes and recited the speech he knew so well. 'If you don't have these rabbits, the monkey, the parakeets, everything, out by sundown, it's the Black Maria for you.'

Mr Pietro nodded with each word, smiling, alert. 'What have I done? Have I murdered a man? Have I kicked a child? Have I stolen a watch? Have I foreclosed a mortgage? Have I bombed a city? Have I fired a gun? Have I told a lie? Have I cheated a customer? Have I turned from the Good Lord? Have I taken a bribe? Have I peddled dope? Do I sell innocent women?'

'No, of course not.'

'Tell me, then, what have I done? Point to it, lay a hand on it. My dogs, these are evil, eh? These birds, their song is dreadful, eh? My phonograph – I suppose that's bad, too, eh? All right, put me in jail, throw away the key. You will not separate us.'

The music rose to a great crescendo. He sang along with it:

> *Tiffa-nee! Hear my plea!*
> *Can't you smile; sit awhile, be my friend?*

The dogs leaped about, barking.

Mr Tiffany drove away in his car.

Pietro felt a pain in his chest. Still grinning, he stopped dancing. The geese rushed in and pecked gently at his shoes as he stood, bent down, holding his chest.

At lunchtime, Pietro opened a quart of homemade Hungarian goulash and refreshed himself. He paused and touched his chest, but the familiar pain had vanished. Finishing his meal, he went to gaze over the high wooden fence in the backyard.

There she was! There was Mrs Gutierrez, very fat, and

as loud as a jukebox, talking to her neighbors on the other side of the lot.

'Lovely lady!' called Mr Massinello Pietro. 'Tonight I go to jail! Your war is fought and won. I give you my saber, my heart, my soul!'

Mrs Gutierrez came ponderously across the dirt yard. 'What?' she said, as if she couldn't see or hear him.

'You told the police, the police told *me*, and I laughed!' His hand flirted on the air, two fingers wiggling. 'I hope you will be happy!'

'I didn't call no police!' she said indignantly.

'Ah, Mrs Gutierrez, I will write a song for you!'

'All of them other people must've called in,' she insisted.

'And when I leave today for jail, I'll have a present for you.' He bowed.

'I tell you it wasn't me!' she cried. 'You and your mealy mouth!'

'I compliment you,' he said sincerely. 'You are a civic-minded citizen. All filth, all noise, all odd things must go.'

'You, you!' she shouted. 'Oh, *you*!' She had no more words.

'I dance for you!' he sang, and waltzed into the house.

In the late afternoon he put on his red silk bandanna and the huge gold earrings and the red sash and the blue vest with the golden piping. He put on his buckle shoes and tight knee breeches. 'Come along! One last walk, eh?' he told his dogs, and out of the shop they went, Pietro carrying the portable phonograph under his arm, wincing with the weight of it, for his stomach and body had been sick for some time and there was something wrong; he couldn't lift things very easily. The dogs padded on either side of him, the parakeets shrieked wildly on his shoulder. The sun was low, the air cool and settled. He looked at everything as if it was new. He said good evening to everyone, he waved, he saluted.

In a hamburger stand he set the phonograph whirling and scratching out the song on top of a stool. People turned to watch as he dived into the song and came up shining with laughter. He snapped his fingers, dipped his legs, whistled sweetly, eyes closed, as the symphony orchestra soared through Strauss. He made the dogs stand in a row while he danced. He made the parakeets tumble on the floor. He caught the spinning, flashing dimes from the startled but responsive audience.

'Get the hell out!' said the hamburger man. 'What in hell you think this is, the opera?'

'Thank you, good friends!' Dogs, music, parakeets, Pietro ran into the night, bells chiming softly.

On a street corner he sang to the sky, to the new stars, and the October moon. A night wind arose. Faces watched smiling from the shadows. Again Pietro winked, smiled, whistled, whirled.

For charity, the poor!
Ah sweet, ah demure!

And he saw all the faces, the looking faces. And he saw the silent houses, with their silent people. And, in his singing, he wondered why he was the last one singing in the world. Why did no one else dance, open mouths, wink, strut, flourish? Why was the world a silent world, silent housed, silent faced? Why were all the people watching people instead of dancing people? Why were they all spectators and only he the performer? What had they forgotten that he always and always remembered? Their houses, small and locked and silent, soundless. His house, his Manger, his shop, different! Filled with squeaks and stirs and mutters of bird sound, filled with feather whisper and murmurings of pad and fur and the sound that animal eyelids make blinking in the dark. His house, ablaze with votive candles and pictures of rising – flying – saints, the glint of medallions. His phonograph circling at midnight, two, three, four in the morning, himself singing, mouth wide, heart open, eyes tight, world shut out; nothing but sound. And here he was now among the houses that locked at nine, slept at ten, wakened only from long silenced hours of slumber in the morn. People in houses, lacking only black wreaths on door fronts.

Sometimes, when he ran by, people remembered for a moment. Sometimes they squeaked a note or two, or tapped their feet, self-consciously, but most of the time the only motion they made to the music was to reach in their pockets for a dime.

Once, thought Pietro, once I had many dimes, many dollars, much land, many houses. And it all went away, and I wept myself into a statue. For a long time I couldn't move. They killed me dead, taking away and taking away. And I thought, I won't ever let anyone kill me again. But how? What do I have that I can let people take away without hurting? What can I give that I still keep?

And the answer was, of course, his talent.

My talent! thought Pietro. The more you give away, the better it is, the more you have. Those with talent must mind the world.

He glanced around. The world was full of statues much like he had been once. So many could move no longer, knew no way to even begin to move again in any direction, back, forth, up, down, for life had stung and bit and stunned and beat them to marble silence. So then, if they could not move, someone must move for them. You, Pietro, he thought, must move. And besides, in moving, you don't look back at what you were or what happened to you or the statue you became. So keep running and keep so busy you can make up for all those with good feet who have forgotten how to run. Run among the self-monuments with bread and flowers. Maybe they will move enough to stoop, touch the flowers, put bread in their dry mouths. And if you shout and sing, they may even talk again someday, and someday fill out the rest of the song with you. Hey! you cry and La! you sing, and dance, and in dancing perhaps their toes may crack and knuckle and bunch and then tap and tremble and someday a long time after, alone in their rooms, because you danced they will dance by themselves in the mirror of their own souls. For remember, once you were chipped out of ice and stone like them, fit for display in a fish-grotto window. But then you shouted and sang at your insides and one of your eyes blinked! Then the other! Then you sighed in a breath and exhaled a great cry of Life! and trembled a finger and shuffled a foot and bounded back into the explosion of life!

Since then, have you ever stopped running?

Never.

Now he ran into a tenement and left white bottles of milk by strange doors. Outside, by a blind beggar on the hurrying street, he carefully placed a folded dollar bill into the lifted cup so quietly that not even the antennae fingers of the old man sensed the tribute. Pietro ran on, thinking, Wine in the cup and he doesn't *know* . . . ha! . . . but, later, he will drink! And running with his dogs and birds flickering, fluttering his shoulders, bells chiming on his shirt, he put flowers by old Widow Villanazul's door, and in the street again paused by the warm bakery window.

The woman who owned the bakery saw him, waved,

and stepped out the door with a hot doughnut in her hand.

'Friend,' she said, 'I wish l had your pep.'

'Madam,' he confessed, biting into the doughnut, nodding his thanks, 'only mind over matter allows me to sing!' He kissed her hand. 'Farewell.' He cocked his alpine hat, did one more dance, and suddenly fell down.

'You should spend a day or two in the hospital.'

'No, I'm conscious; and you can't put me in the hospital unless I say so,' said Pietro. 'I have to get home. People are waiting for me.'

'Okay,' said the intern.

Pietro took his newspaper clippings from his pocket. 'Look at these. Pictures of me in court, with my pets. Are my dogs here?' he cried in sudden concern, looking wildly about.

'Yes.'

The dogs rustled and whined under the cot. The parakeets pecked at the intern every time his hand wandered over Pietro's chest.

The intern read the news clippings. 'Hey, that's all right.'

'I sang for the *judge*, they couldn't stop me!' said Pietro, eyes closed, enjoying the ride, the hum, the rush. His head joggled softly. The sweat ran on his face, erasing the makeup, making the lampblack run in wriggles from his eyebrows and temples, showing the white hair underneath.

His bright cheeks drained in rivulets away, leaving pale-
ness. The intern swabbed pink color off with cotton.

'*Here* we are!' called the driver.

'What time is it?' As the ambulance stopped and the
back doors flipped wide, Pietro took the intern's wrist to
peer at the gold watch. 'Five-thirty! I haven't much time;
they'll be here!'

'Take it easy, you all right?' The intern balanced him
on the oily street in front of the Manger.

'Fine, fine,' said Pietro, winking. He pinched the
intern's arm. 'Thank you.'

With the ambulance gone, he unlocked the Manger
and the warm animal smells mingled around him.
Other dogs, all wool, bounded to lick him. The geese
waddled in, pecked bitterly at his ankles until he did
a dance of pain, waddled out, honking like pressed
horn-bulbs.

He glanced at the empty street. Any minute, yes, any
minute. He took the lovebirds from their perches.
Outside, in the darkened yard, he called over the fence,
'Mrs Gutierrez!' When she loomed in the moonlight, he
placed the lovebirds in her fat hands. 'For you, Mrs
Gutierrez!'

'What?' She squinted at the things in her hands,
turning them. 'What?'

'Take good care of them!' he said. 'Feed them and
they will sing for you!'

'What can I do with these?' she wondered, looking

at the sky, at him, at the birds. 'Oh, please.' She was helpless.

He patted her arm. 'I know you will be good to them.'

The back door to the Manger slammed.

In the following hour he gave one of the geese to Mr Gomez, one to Felipe Diaz, a third to Mrs Florianna. A parrot he gave to Mr Brown, the grocer up the street. And the dogs, separately, and in sorrow, he put into the hands of passing children.

At seven-thirty a car cruised around the block twice before stopping. Mr Tiffany finally came to the door and looked in. 'Well,' he said. 'I see you're getting rid of them. Half of them gone, eh? I'll give you another hour, since you're cooperating. That's the boy.'

'No,' said Mr Pietro, standing there, looking at the empty crates. 'I will give no more away.'

'Oh, but look here,' said Tiffany. 'You don't want to go to jail for these few remaining. Let my boys take these out for you—'

'Lock me up!' said Pietro. 'I am ready!'

He reached down and took the portable phonograph and put it under his arm. He checked his face in a cracked mirror. The lampblack was reapplied, his white hair gone. The mirror floated in space, hot, misshapen. He was beginning to drift, his feet hardly touched the floor. He was feverish, his tongue thick. He heard himself saying, 'Let us go.'

Tiffany stood with his open hands out, as if to prevent

Pietro from going anywhere. Pietro stooped down, swaying. The last slick brown dachshund coiled into his arm, like a little soft tire, pink tongue licking.

'You can't take that dog,' said Tiffany, incredulous.

'Just to the station, just for the ride?' asked Pietro. He was tired now; tiredness was in each finger, each limb, in his body, in his head.

'All right,' said Tiffany. 'God, you make things tough.'

Pietro moved out of the shop, dog and phonograph under either arm. Tiffany took the key from Pietro. 'We'll clean out the animals later,' he said.

'Thanks,' said Pietro, 'for not doing it while I'm here.'

'Ah, for God's sake,' said Tiffany.

Everyone was on the street, watching. Pietro shook his dog at them, like a man who has just won a battle and is holding up clenched hands in victory.

'Good-bye, good-bye! I don't know where I'm going but I'm on my way! This is a very sick man. But I'll be back! Here I go!' He laughed, and waved.

They climbed into the police car. He held the dog to one side, the phonograph on his lap. He cranked it and started it. The phonograph was playing 'Tales from the Vienna Woods' as the car drove away.

On either side of the Manger that night it was quiet at one A.M. and it was quiet at two A.M. and it was quiet at three A.M. and it was such a *loud* quietness at four A.M. that everyone blinked, sat up in bed, and *listened*.

The Visit

Ray Bradbury
October 20, 1984
9:45–10:07
(On reading about a young actor's death and his heart placed in another man's body last night.)

She had called and there was to be a visit.

At first the young man had been reluctant, had said no, no thanks, he was sorry, he understood, but no.

But then when he heard her silence on the other end of the telephone, no sound at all, but the kind of grief which keeps to itself, he had waited a long while and then said, yes, all right, come over, but, please, don't stay too long. This is a strange situation and I don't know how to handle it.

Nor did she. Going to the young man's apartment, she wondered what she would say and how she would react, and what he would say. She was terribly afraid of doing something so emotional that he would have to push her out of the apartment and slam the door.

For she didn't know this young man at all. He was a total and complete stranger. They had never met and only yesterday she had found his name at last, after a desperate search through friends at a local hospital. And now, before it was too late, she simply had to visit a totally unknown person for the most peculiar reasons in all her life or, for that matter, in the lives of all mothers in the world since civilization began.

'Please wait.'

She gave the cabdriver a twenty-dollar bill to ensure his being there should she come out sooner than she expected, and stood at the entrance to the apartment building for a long moment before she took a deep breath, opened the door, went in, and took the elevator up to the third floor.

She shut her eyes outside his door, and took another deep breath and knocked. There was no answer. With sudden panic, she knocked very hard. This time, at last, the door opened.

The young man, somewhere between twenty and twenty-four, looked timidly out at her and said, 'You're Mrs Hadley?'

'You don't look like him at all,' she heard herself say.

'I mean—' She caught herself and flushed and almost turned to go away.

'You didn't really expect me to, did you?'

He opened the door wider and stepped aside. There was coffee waiting on a small table in the center of the apartment.

'No, no, silly. I didn't know what I was saying.'

'Sit down, please. I'm William Robinson. Bill to you, I guess. Black or white?'

'Black.' And she watched him pour.

'How did you find me?' he said, handing the cup over.

She took it with trembling fingers. 'I know some people at the hospital. They did some checking.'

'They shouldn't have.'

'Yes, I know. But I kept at them. You see, I'm going away to live in France for a year, maybe more. This was my last chance to visit my – I mean—'

She lapsed into silence and stared into the coffee cup.

'So they put two and two together, even though the files were supposed to be locked?' he said quietly.

'Yes,' she said. 'It all came together. The night my son died was the same night you were brought into the hospital for a heart transplant. It had to be you. There was no other operation like that that night or that week. I knew that when you left the hospital, my son, his heart anyway' – she had difficulty saying it – 'went with you.' She put down the coffee cup.

'I don't know why I'm here,' she said.

'Yes, you do,' he said.

'Not really, I don't. It's all so strange and sad and terrible and at the same time, I don't know, God's gift. Does that make any sense?'

'To me it does. I'm alive because of the gift.'

Now it was his turn to fall silent, pour himself coffee, stir it and drink.

'When you leave here,' said the young man, 'where will you go?'

'Go?' said the woman uncertainly.

'I mean—' The young man winced with his own lack of ease. The words simply would not come. 'I mean, have you other visits to make? Are there other—'

'I see.' The woman nodded several times, took hold of herself with a motion of her body, looking at her hands in her lap, and at last shrugged. 'Yes, there are others. My son, his vision was given to someone in Oregon. There is someone else in Tucson—'

'You don't have to continue,' said the young man. 'I shouldn't have asked.'

'No, no. It is all so strange, so ridiculous. It is all so new. Just a few years ago, nothing like this could have happened. Now we're in a new time. I don't know whether to laugh or cry. Sometimes I start one and then do the other. I wake up confused. I often wonder if he is confused. But that's even sillier. He is nowhere.'

'He is somewhere,' said the young man. 'He is here. And I'm alive because he is here at this very moment.'

The woman's eyes grew very bright, but no tears fell. 'Yes. Thank you for that.'

'No, I thank him, and you for allowing me to live.'

The woman jumped up suddenly, as if propelled by an emotion stronger than she knew. She looked around for the perfectly obvious door and seemed not to see it.

'Where are you going?'

'I—' she said.

'You just got here!'

'This is stupid!' she cried. 'Embarrassing. I'm putting too much of a burden on you, on myself. I'm going now before it all gets so ludicrous I go mad—'

'Stay,' said the young man.

Obedient to the command, she almost sat down.

'Finish your coffee.'

She remained standing, but picked up her coffee cup with shaking hands. The soft rattle of the cup was the only sound for a time as she slaked the coffee with some unquenchable thirst. Then she put the empty cup down and said: 'I really must go. I feel faint. I feel I might fall down. I am so embarrassed with myself, with coming here. God bless you, young man, and may you have a long life.'

She started toward the door, but he stood in her way.

'Do what you came to do,' he said.

'What, what?'

'You know. You know very well. I won't mind it. Do it.'

'I—'

'Go on,' he said gently, and shut his eyes, his hands at his side, waiting.

She stared into his face and then at his chest, where under his shirt there seemed the gentlest stirring.

'Now,' he said quietly.

She almost moved.

'Now,' he said, for a final time.

She took one step forward. She turned her head and quietly moved her right ear down and then again down, inch by inch, until it touched the young man's chest.

She might have cried out, but did not. She might have exclaimed something, but did not. Her eyes were also shut now and she was listening. Her lips moved, saying something, perhaps a name, over and over, almost to the rhythm of the pulse she heard under the shirt, under the flesh, within the body of the patient young man.

The heart was beating there.

She listened.

The heart beat with a steady and regular sound.

She listened for a long while. Her breath slowly drained out of her, as color came into her cheeks.

She listened.

The heart beat.

Then she raised her head, looked at the young man's face for a final time, and very swiftly touched her lips to his cheek, turned, and hurried across the room, with no thanks, for none was needed. At the door she did not even turn around but opened it and went out and closed the door softly.

The young man waited for a long moment. His right hand came up and slid across his shirt, across his chest to feel what lay underneath. His eyes were still shut and his face emotionless.

Then he turned and sat down without looking where he sat and picked up his coffee cup to finish his coffee.

The strong pulse, the great vibration of the life within his chest, traveled along his arm and into the cup and caused it to pulse in a steady rhythm, unending, as he placed it against his lips, and drank the coffee as if it were a medicine, a gift, that would refill the cup again and again through more days than he could possibly guess or see. He drained the cup.

Only then did he open his eyes and see that the room was empty.

The Twilight Greens

It was getting late, but he thought there was just enough sunlight left that he could play a quick nine holes before he had to stop.

But even as he drove toward the golf course twilight came. A high fog had drifted in from the ocean, erasing the light.

He was about to turn away when something caught his eye.

Gazing out at the far meadows, he saw a half dozen or so golfers playing in the shadowed fields.

The players were not in foursomes, but walked singly, carrying their clubs across the grass, moving under the trees.

How strange, he thought. And, instead of leaving, he drove into the lot behind the clubhouse and got out.

Something made him go stand and watch a few men at the driving range, clubbing the golf balls to send them sailing out into the twilight.

But still those lone strollers far out on the fairway made him immensely curious; there was a certain melancholy to the scene.

Almost without thinking, he picked up his bag and carried his golf clubs out to the first tee, where three old men stood as if waiting for him.

Old men, he thought. Well no, not exactly old, but he was only thirty and they were well on into turning gray.

When he arrived they gazed at his suntanned face and his sharp clear eyes.

One of the aging men said hello.

'What's going on?' said the young man, though he wondered why he asked it that way.

He studied the fields and the single golfers moving away in the shadows.

'I mean,' he said, nodding toward the fairway, 'you'd think they'd be heading in. In ten minutes they won't be able to see.'

'They'll see, all right,' said one of the older men. 'Fact is, *we're* going out. We like the late hour, it's a chance to be alone and think about things. So we'll start off in a group and then go our separate ways.'

'That's a hell of a thing to do,' said the young man.

'So it is,' said the other. 'But we have our reasons.

Come along if you want, but when we're out about a hundred yards, you'll most likely find yourself alone.'

The young man thought about it and nodded.

'It's a deal,' he said.

One by one they stepped up to the tee and swung their clubs and watched the white golf balls vanish into the half dark.

They walked out into the last light, quietly.

The old man walked with the young man, occasionally glancing over at him. The other two men only looked ahead and said nothing. When they stopped the young man gasped. The old man said, 'What?'

The young man exclaimed, 'My God, I *found* it! How come, in this lousy light, I somehow *knew* where it would be?'

'Those things happen,' said the old man. 'You could call it fate, or luck, or Zen. I call it simple, pure need. Go ahead.'

The young man looked down at his golf ball lying on the grass and stepped back quietly.

'No, the others first,' he said.

The other two men had also found their white golf balls lying in the grass and now took turns. One swung and hit and walked off alone. The other swung and hit and then he, too, vanished in the twilight.

The young man watched them going their separate ways.

'I don't understand,' he said. 'I've never played in a foursome like this.'

'It's really not a foursome,' said the old man. 'You might call it a variation. They'll go on and we'll all meet again at the nineteenth green. Your turn.'

The young man hit and the ball sailed off into the purple-gray sky. He could almost hear it hit the grass a hundred yards out.

'Go on,' said the old man.

'No,' said the young man. 'If you don't mind, I'll walk with you.'

The old man nodded, positioned himself, and hit his golf ball into the dark. Then they walked on together in silence.

At last the young man, staring ahead, trying to figure the beginning night, said, 'I've never seen a game played this way. Who are those others and what are they doing here? For that matter, who are you? And finally, I wonder, what in hell am I doing here? I don't fit.'

'Not quite,' said the old man. 'But perhaps someday you will.'

'Someday?' said the young man. 'If I don't fit now, why not?'

The old man kept walking, looking ahead, but not over at the younger man.

'You're much too young,' he said. 'How old are you?'

'Thirty,' said the young man.

'That's young. Wait until you're fifty or sixty. Then maybe you'll be ready to play the Twilight Greens.'

'Is that what you call it, the Twilight Greens?'

'Yes,' said the old man. 'Sometimes fellows like us go out and play really late, don't come in till seven or eight o'clock; we have that need to just hit the ball and walk and hit again, then head in when we're really tired.'

'How do you know,' said the young man, 'when you're ready to play the Twilight Greens?'

'Well,' said the old man, walking quietly, 'we're widowers. Not the usual kind. Everyone has heard of golf widows, women who are left at home when their husbands play golf all day Sunday, sometimes on Saturday, sometimes during the week; they get so caught up in it that they can't quit. They become golfing machines and the wives wonder where in hell their husbands went. Well, in this case, we call ourselves the widowers; the wives are still at home, but the homes are cold, nobody lights a fire, meals are cooked, though not very often, and the beds are half empty. The widowers.'

The young man said, 'Widowers? I still don't quite understand. Nobody's dead, are they?'

'No,' the old man said. 'When you say "golf widows," it means women left at home when men go out to play golf. In this case, "widowers" means men who have in fact widowed themselves from their homes.'

The young man mused for a moment and then said, 'But there are people at home? There is a woman in each house, yes?'

'Oh yes,' said the old man. 'They are there. They are there. But . . .'

'But what?' said the young man.

'Well, look at it this way,' said the old man, still walking quietly and looking off into the Twilight Greens. 'For whatever reason, we come here at twilight, onto the fairway. Maybe because at home there is too little talk, or too much. Too much pillow talk, or too little. Too many children, or not enough children, or no children at all. All sorts of excuses. Too much money, not enough. Whatever the reason, all of a sudden these loners here have discovered that a good place to be as the sun goes down is out on the fairway, playing alone, hitting the ball, and following it into the fading light.'

'I see,' said the young man.

'I'm not quite sure that you do.'

'No,' said the young man, 'I do indeed, I do indeed. But I don't think I'll ever come back here again at twilight.'

The old man looked at him and nodded.

'No, I don't think you will. Not for a while, anyway. Maybe in twenty or thirty years. You've got too good a suntan and you walk too quickly and you look like you're all revved up. From now on you should arrive here at noon and play with a real foursome. You shouldn't be out here, walking on the Twilight Greens.'

'I'll *never* come back at night,' said the young man. 'It will *never* happen to me.'

'I hope not,' said the old man.

'I'll make sure of it,' said the young man. 'I think I've walked as far as I need to walk. I think that last hit put my ball too far out in the dark; I don't think I want to find it.'

'Well said,' said the old man.

And they walked back and the night was really gathering now and they couldn't hear their footsteps in the grass.

Behind them the lone strollers still moved, some in, some out, along the far greens.

When they reached the clubhouse, the young man looked at the old, who seemed very old indeed, and the old man looked at the young, who looked very young indeed.

'If you do come back,' said the old man, 'at twilight, that is, if you ever feel the need to play a round starting out with three others and winding up alone, there's one thing I've got to warn you about.'

'What's that?' said the young man.

'There is one word you must never use when you converse with all those people who wander out along the evening grass prairie.'

'And the word is?' said the young man.

'Marriage,' whispered the old man.

He shook the young man's hand, took his bag of clubs, and walked away.

Far out, on the Twilight Greens, it now was true dark, and you could not see the men who still played there.

The young man with his suntanned face and clear, bright eyes turned, walked to his car, and drove away.

The Murder

'There are some people who would never commit a murder,' said Mr Bentley.

'Who, for instance?' said Mr Hill.

'Me, for instance, and lots more like me,' said Mr Bentley.

'Poppycock!' said Mr Hill.

'Poppycock?'

'You heard what I said. Everybody's capable of murder. Even you.'

'I haven't a motive in the world, I'm content with things, my wife is a good woman, I've got enough money, a good job, why should I commit murder?' said Mr Bentley.

'I could make you commit murder,' said Mr Hill.

'You could *not*.'

'I could.' Mr Hill looked out over the small green summer town, meditatively.

'You can't make a murderer out of a nonmurderer.'

'Yes, I could.'

'No, you couldn't!'

'How much would you like to bet?'

'I've never bet in my life. Don't believe in it.'

'Oh, hell, a gentleman's bet,' said Mr Hill. 'A dollar. A dollar to a dime. Come on, now, you'd bet a dime, wouldn't you? You'd be three kinds of Scotchman not to, and showing little faith in your thesis, besides. Isn't it worth a dime to prove you're not a murderer?'

'You're joking.'

'We're both joking and we're both not. All I'm interested in proving is that you're no different than any other man. You've got a button to be pushed. If I could find it and push it, you'd commit murder.'

Mr Bentley laughed easily and cut the end from a cigar, twirled it between his comfortably fleshy lips, and leaned back in his rocker. Then he fumbled in his unbuttoned vest pocket, found a dime, and laid it on the porch newel in front of him. 'All right,' he said, and, thinking, drew forth another dime. 'There's twenty cents says I'm not a murderer. Now how are you going to prove that I am?' He chuckled and squeezed his eyes deliciously shut. 'I'm going to be sitting around here a good many years.'

'There'll be a time limit, of course.'

'Oh, *will* there?' Bentley laughed still louder.

'Yes. One month from today, you'll be a murderer.'

'One month from today, eh? Ho!' And he laughed, because the idea was so patently ridiculous. Recovering enough, he put his tongue in his cheek. 'Today's August first, right? So on September first, you owe me a dollar.'

'No, you'll owe me two dimes.'

'You're stubborn, aren't you?'

'You don't know how stubborn.'

It was a fine late-summer evening, with just the right breeze, a lack of mosquitoes, two cigars burning the right way, and the sound of Mr Bentley's wife clashing the dinner plates into soapsuds in the distant kitchen. Along the streets of the small town, people were coming out onto their porches, nodding at one another.

'This is one of the most foolish conversations I've ever held in my life,' said Mr Bentley, sniffing the air with glad appreciation, noting the smell of fresh-cut grass. 'We talk about murder for ten minutes, we get off into whether all of us are capable of murder, and, next thing you know, we've made a bet.'

'Yes,' said Mr Hill.

Mr Bentley looked over at his boarder. Mr Hill was about fifty-five, though he looked a bit older, with cold blue eyes, and a gray face, and lines that made it look like an apricot that has been allowed to shrivel in the sun. He was neatly bald, like a Caesar, and had an intense way of talking, gripping the chair, gripping your arm,

gripping his own hands together as if in prayer, always
convincing himself or convincing you of the truth of his
exclamations. They had had many good talks in the past
three months, since Mr Hill had moved into the back
bedroom. They had talked of myriad things: locusts in
spring, snow in April, seasonal tempests and coolings,
trips to far places, the usual talk, scented with tobacco,
comfortable as a full dinner, and there was a feeling in
Mr Bentley that he had grown up with this stranger,
known him from his days as a yelling child through
bumpy adolescence to whitening senility. This, come to
think of it, was the first time they had ever disagreed
on anything. The wonderful thing about their friendship
had been that it had so far excluded any quibblings or
side issues, and had walked the straight way of Truth,
or what the two men thought was truth, or perhaps,
thought Mr Bentley now, with the cigar in his hand,
what he had thought was the truth and what Mr Hill,
out of politeness or plan, had pretended to take for the
truth also.

'Easiest money I ever made,' said Mr Bentley.

'Wait and see. Carry those dimes with you. You may
need them soon.'

Mr Bentley put the coins into his vest pocket, half
soberly. Perhaps a turn in the wind had, for a moment,
changed the temperature of his thoughts. For a moment, his
mind said, Well, could you murder? Eh?

'Shake on it,' said Mr Hill.

Mr Hill's cold hand gripped tightly.

'It's a bet.'

'All right, you fat slob, good night,' said Mr Hill, and got up.

'What?' cried Mr Bentley, startled, not insulted yet, but because he couldn't believe that terrible use of words.

'Good night, slob,' said Mr Hill, looking at him calmly. His hands were busy, moving aside the buttons on his summer shirt. The flesh of his lean stomach was revealed. There was an old scar there. It looked as if a bullet had gone cleanly through.

'You see,' said Mr Hill, seeing the wide popping eyes of the plump man in the rocking chair, 'I've made this bet before.'

The front door shut softly. Mr Hill was gone.

The light was burning in Mr Hill's room at ten minutes after one. Sitting there in the dark, Mr Bentley at last, unable to find sleep, got up and moved softly into the hall and looked at Mr Hill. For the door was open and there was Mr Hill standing before a mirror, touching, tapping, pinching himself, now here, now there.

And he seemed to be thinking to himself, Look at me! Look, here, Bentley, and *here*!

Bentley looked.

There were three round scars on Hill's chest and stomach. There was a long slash scar over his heart, and a little one on his neck. And on his back, as if a dragon had pulled its talons across in a furious raveling, a series of terrible furrows.

Mr Bentley stood with his tongue between his lips, his hands open.

'Come in,' said Mr Hill.

Bentley did not move.

'You're up late.'

'Just looking at myself. Vanity, vanity.'

'Those scars, all those scars.'

'There are a few, aren't there?'

'So many. My God, I've never seen scars like that. How did you get them?'

Hill went on preening and feeling and caressing himself, stripped to the waist. 'Well, now maybe you can guess.' He winked and smiled friendlily.

'How did you get them?!'

'You'll wake your wife.'

'Tell me!'

'Use your imagination, man.'

He exhaled and inhaled and exhaled again.

'What can I do for you, Mr Bentley?'

'I've come—'

'Speak up.'

'I want you to move out.'

'Oh now, Bentley.'

'We need this room.'

'Really?'

'My wife's mother is coming to visit.'

'That's a lie.'

Bentley nodded. 'Yes. I'm lying.'

'Why don't you say it? You want me to leave, period.'

'Right.'

'Because you're afraid of me.'

'No, I'm not afraid.'

'Well, what if I told you I wouldn't leave?'

'No, you couldn't do that.'

'Well, I could, and I am.'

'No, no.'

'What are we having for breakfast, ham and eggs again?'
He craned his neck to examine that little scar there.

'Please say you'll go,' asked Mr Bentley.

'No,' said Mr Hill.

'Please.'

'There's no use begging. You make yourself look silly.'

'Well, then, if you stay here, let's call off the bet.'

'Why call it off?'

'Because.'

'Afraid of yourself?'

'No, I'm not!'

'Shh.' He pointed to the wall. 'Your wife.'

'Let's call off the bet. Here. Here's my money. You
win!' He groped frantically into his pocket and drew
forth the two dimes. He threw them on the dresser,
crashing. 'Take them! You win! I could commit murder,
I could, I admit it.'

Mr Hill waited a moment, and without looking at the

coins, put his fingers down on the dresser, groped, found them, picked them up, clinked them, held them out. 'Here.'

'I don't want them back!' Bentley retreated to the doorway.

'Take them.'

'You win!'

'A bet is a bet. This proves nothing.'

He turned and came to Bentley and dropped them in Bentley's shirt pocket and patted them. Bentley took two steps back into the hall. 'I do not make bets idly,' Hill said.

Bentley stared at those terrible scars. 'How many other people have you made this bet with!' he cried. 'How many?!'

Hill laughed. 'Ham and eggs, eh?'

'How many?! How many?!'

'See you at breakfast,' said Mr Hill.

He shut the door. Mr Bentley stood looking at it. He could see the scars through the door, as if by some translucency of the eye and mind. The razor scars. The knife scars. They hung in the paneling, like knots in old wood.

The light went out behind the door.

He stood over the body and he heard the house waking up, rushing, the feet down the stairs, the shouts, the half screams and stirrings. In a moment, people would be flooding around him. In a moment, there'd be a siren and a flashing red light, the car doors slamming, the snap of manacles to the fleshy wrists, the questions, the peering into his white, bewildered face. But now he only stood over the body, fumbling. The gun had fallen into the deep, good-smelling night grass. The air was still charged with electricity but the storm was passing, and he was beginning to notice things again. And there was his right hand, all by itself, fumbling about like a blind mole, digging, digging senselessly at his shirt pocket until it found what it wanted. And he felt his gross weight bend, stoop, almost fall, as he almost rushed down over the body. His blind hand went out and closed the up-staring eyes of Mr Hill, and on each wrinkled, cooling eyelid put a shiny new dime.

The door slammed behind him. Hattie screamed.

He turned to her with a sick smile. 'I just lost a bet,' he heard himself say.

When the Bough Breaks

The night was cold and there was a slight wind which
had begun to rise around two in the morning.

The leaves in all the trees outside began to tremble.

By three o'clock the wind was constant and murmuring
outside the window.

She was the first to open her eyes.

And then, for some imperceptible reason, he stirred
in his half sleep.

'You awake?' he said.

'Yes,' she said. 'There was a sound, something called.'

He half raised his head.

A long way off there was a soft wailing.

'Hear that?' she asked.

'What?'

'Something's crying.'

'Something?' he said.

'Someone,' she said. 'It sounds like a ghost.'

'My God, what a thing. What time is it?'

'Three in the morning. That terrible hour.'

'Terrible?' he said.

'You know Dr Meade told us at the hospital that that's the one hour when people just give up, they don't keep trying anymore. That's when they die. Three in the morning.'

'I'd rather not think about that,' he said.

The sound from outside the house grew louder.

'There it is again,' she said. 'That sounds like a ghost.'

'Oh my God,' he whispered. 'What kind of ghost?'

'A baby,' she said. 'A baby crying.'

'Since when do babies have ghosts? Have we known any babies recently that died?' He made a soft sound of laughter.

'No,' she said, and shook her head back and forth. 'But maybe it's not the ghost of a baby that died, but . . . I don't know. Listen.'

He listened and the crying came again, a long way off.

'What if—' she said.

'Yes?'

'What if it's the ghost of a child—'

'Go on,' he said.

'That hasn't been born yet.'

'Are there such ghosts? And can they make sounds? My God, why do I say that? What a strange thing to say.'

'The ghost of a baby that hasn't been born yet.'

'How can it have a voice?' he said.

'Maybe it's not dead, but just wants to live,' she said. 'It's so far off, so sad. How can we answer it?'

They both listened and the quiet cry continued and the wind wailed outside the window.

Listening, tears came into her eyes and, listening, the same thing happened to him.

'I can't stand this,' he said. 'I'm going to get up and get something to eat.'

'No, no,' she said, and took his hand and held it. 'Be very quiet and listen. Maybe we'll get answers.'

He lay back and held her hand and tried to shut his eyes, but could not.

They both lay in bed and the wind continued murmuring, and the leaves shook outside the window.

A long way off, a great distance off, the sound of weeping went on and on.

'Who could that be?' she said. '*What* could that be? It won't stop. It makes me so sad. Is it asking to be let in?'

'Let in?' he said.

'To live. It's not dead, it's never lived, but it wants to live. Do you think—' She hesitated.

'What?'

'Oh my God,' she said. 'Do you think the way we talked a month ago . . . ?'

'What talk was that?' he said.

'About the future. About our not having a family. No family. No *children*.'

'I don't remember,' he said.

'Try to,' she said. 'We promised each other no family, no children.' She hesitated and then added, 'No babies.'

'No children. No babies?'

'Do you think—' She raised her head and listened to the crying outside the window, far away, through the trees, across the country. 'Can it be that—'

'What?' he said.

'I think,' she said, 'that I know a way to stop that crying.'

He waited for her to continue.

'I think that maybe—'

'What?' he said.

'Maybe you should come over on this side of the bed.'

'Are you asking me over?'

'I am, yes, please, come over.'

He turned and looked at her and finally rolled completely over toward her. A long way off the town clock struck three-fifteen, then three-thirty, then three forty-five, then four o'clock.

Then they both lay, listening.

'Do you hear?' she said.

'I'm listening.'

'The crying.'

'It's stopped,' he said.

'Yes. That ghost, that child, that baby, that crying, thank God it stopped.'

He held her hand, turned his face toward her, and said, 'We stopped it.'

'We did,' she said. 'Oh yes, thank God, we stopped it.'

The night was very quiet. The wind began to die. The leaves on the trees outside stopped trembling.

And they lay in the night, hand in hand, listening to the silence, the wonderful silence, and waited for the dawn.

We'll Always Have Paris

It was a hot Saturday night in July in Paris, near midnight, when I prepared to head out and walk around the city, my favorite pastime, starting at Notre Dame and ending, sometimes, at the Eiffel Tower.

My wife had gone to bed at nine o'clock and as I stood by the door she said, 'No matter how late, bring back some pizza.'

'One pizza coming up,' I said, and stepped out into the hall.

I walked from the hotel across the river and along to Notre Dame and then stopped in at the Shakespeare Bookstore and headed back along the Boul Miche to stop at Les Deux Magots, the outdoor café where Hemingway, more than a generation ago, had regaled his friends with Pernod, grappa, and Africa.

I sat there for a while watching the Parisians, of which there was a multitude, had myself a Pernod and a beer, and then headed back toward the river.

The street leading away from Les Deux Magots was no more than an alley lined with antiques stores and art galleries.

I walked along, almost alone, and was nearing the Seine when a peculiar thing happened, the strangest thing that had ever happened in my life.

I realized I was being followed. But it was a strange kind of following.

I looked behind me and no one was there. I looked ahead about forty yards and saw a young man in a summer suit.

At first I didn't realize what he was doing. But when I stopped to look in a window and glanced up, I saw that he had stopped eighty or ninety feet ahead of me and was looking back, watching me.

As soon as he saw my glance he walked away, farther on up the street, where he stopped again and looked back.

After a few more of these silent exchanges, it came to me what was going on. Instead of following me from behind, he was following me by leading the way and looking back to make sure that I came along.

The process continued for an entire city block and then finally, at last, I came to an intersection and found him waiting for me.

He was tall and slender and blond and quite handsome and seemed, somehow, to be French; he looked
athletic, perhaps a tennis player or a swimmer.

I didn't know quite how I felt about the situation.
Was I pleased, was I flattered, was I embarrassed?

Suddenly, confronted with him, I stood at the intersection and said something in English and he shook his
head.

He said something in French and I shook my head
and then both of us laughed.

'No French?' he said.

I shook my head.

'No English?' I said, and he shook his head and, again,
we both laughed because here we were, past midnight
in Paris, at an intersection, unable to talk to each other
and not quite knowing what we were doing there.

At last, he lifted one hand and pointed off down a
side street.

He said a name and I thought it was the name of
someone: 'Jim.' I shook my head in confusion.

He repeated himself, and then clarified the word.
'Gymnasium,' he said as he pointed again, stepped off
the walk into the street, and turned to see if I was
following.

Hesitant, I waited as he walked full across the street
to the far curb and then turned again and looked at me.

I stepped off the curb and followed, thinking, What
am I doing here? And then, again, What the *hell* am I

doing here? A strange young man at midnight, in hot weather, in Paris, going where? To some strange gymnasium? What if I never come back? I mean, in the middle of a strange city, how come I had the nerve to follow where someone else was leading?

I followed.

In the middle of the next block I found him waiting for me.

He nodded to a nearby building and repeated the word *gymnasium*. I watched as he started down some steps at the side of the building, and ran to follow. Down we went to a basement door that he unlocked and nodded me into the darkness.

I saw that we were indeed in a small gym with all the equipment that such facilities have: workout machines and block horses and mats.

Most peculiar, I thought, and stepped forward as he closed the door.

From the ceiling above I heard distant music and voices speaking and the next thing I knew I felt my shirt being unbuttoned.

I stood in the dark with perspiration running down my arms and off the tip of my nose. I could hear the sounds of his taking off his clothes in the dark as we stood there at midnight in Paris, not moving, not speaking.

Again I thought, What the hell am I doing here?

He took a step forward and almost touched me when suddenly there was the sound of a door opening somewhere nearby, a burst of laughter, another door opening and shutting, and footsteps and people talking very loudly from above.

I jumped at the noise and stood there, trembling.

He must have felt my movement, for he put out his hands, placing one on my left shoulder, one on my right.

Both of us seemed not to know what to do next, but we stood there, facing each other, after midnight, in Paris, like two actors onstage who had forgotten their lines.

From above there was laughter and music and I thought I heard the popping of a cork.

In the dim light I saw a single bead of perspiration slide down and fall off the tip of his nose.

I felt the perspiration slip down my arms and drip off the ends of my fingers.

We stood there for a long time, not moving, when at last he shrugged a French shrug and I shrugged, too, and then we both laughed quietly again.

He bent forward, took my chin in one hand, and planted a quiet kiss in the middle of my brow. Then he stepped back and reached out and put my shirt around my shoulders.

'Bonne chance,' I thought I heard him murmur.

And then we moved quietly to the door and he put his finger to his lips and said, 'Shhhh,' and we both went out into the street.

We walked together back up to the narrow avenue

that led in one direction to Les Deux Magots, and in the
other direction to the river, the Louvre, and my hotel.

'My God,' I said quietly. 'We've been together a half
hour and we don't even know each other's name.'

He looked at me inquiringly and some inspiration
caused me to lift my hand and jab at his chest with my
finger.

'You Jane, me Tarzan,' I said.

This caused him to explode with laughter and repeat
what I had said: 'Me Jane, you Tarzan.'

And for the first time since we met, we both relaxed
and laughed.

Again he leaned forward and planted another quiet
kiss in the middle of my brow, then turned and walked
away.

When he was three or four yards off, without turning
he said, in halting English, 'Sorry.'

I replied, 'Very sorry.'

'Next time?' he said.

'Next,' I replied.

And then he was gone down the narrow street, no
longer leading me.

I turned back toward the river, walked on past the
Louvre, and to my hotel.

It was two o'clock in the morning, still very hot, and
as I stood inside the door to the suite I heard the bedclothes
rustle and my wife said, 'I forgot to ask earlier, did you
get the tickets?'

'Oh yes,' I said. 'The Concorde, noon flight to New York, next Tuesday.'

I heard my wife relax and then she sighed and said, 'My God, I love Paris. I hope we can come back next year.'

'Next year,' I said.

I undressed and sat on the edge of the bed. From the far side my wife said, 'Did you remember the pizza?'

'The pizza?' I said.

'How could you have forgotten the pizza?' she said.

'I don't know,' I said.

I felt a peculiar quiet itch in the middle of my forehead and put my hand up to touch the place where that strange young man who had followed me by leading had kissed me good night.

'I don't know,' I said, 'how I could have forgotten. Damned if I know.'

Ma Perkins Comes to Stay

Joe Tiller entered the apartment and was removing his hat when he saw the middle-aged, plump woman facing him, shelling peas.

'Come in,' she said to his startled face. 'Annie's out fetchin' supper. Set down.'

'But who—' He looked at her.

'I'm Ma Perkins.' She laughed, rocking. It was not a rocking chair, but somehow she imparted the sense of rocking to it. Tiller felt giddy. 'Just call me Ma,' she said airily.

'The name is familiar, but—'

'Never you mind, son. You'll get to know me. I'm staying on a year or so, just visitin'.' And here she laughed comfortably and shelled a green pea.

Tiller rushed out to the kitchen and confronted his wife.

'Who in the hell *is* she, that nasty nice old woman?!' he cried.

'On the radio.' His wife smiled. 'You *know*. Ma *Perkins*.'

'Well, what's she doing here?' he shouted.

'Shh. She's come to help.'

'Help what?' He glared toward the other room.

'Things,' said his wife indefinitely.

'Where'll we put her, damn it? She has to sleep, doesn't she?'

'Oh yes,' said Anna, his wife, sweetly. 'But the radio's right there. At night she just sort of – well – "goes back."'

'Why did she come? Did you write to her? You never told me you knew her,' exclaimed the husband wildly.

'Oh, I've *listened* to her for years,' said Anna.

'That's different.'

'No. I've always felt I knew Ma better almost than I know – you,' said his wife.

He stood confounded. Ten years, he thought. Ten years alone in this chintz cell with her warm radio humming, the pink silver tubes burning, voices murmuring. Ten secret years of monastic conspiracy, radio and women, while he was holding his exploding business together. He decided to be very jovial and reasonable.

'What I want to know is' – he took her hand – 'did you write "Ma" or call her up? How did she *get* here?'

'She's been here ten years.'

'Like hell she has!'

'Well today is *special*,' admitted his wife. 'Today's the first time she's ever *"stayed."'*

He took his wife to the parlor to confront the old woman. 'Get out,' he said.

Ma looked up from dicing some pink carrots and showed her teeth. 'Land, I can't. It's up to Annie, there. You'll have to ask *her*.'

He whirled. 'Well?' he said to his wife.

His wife's face was cold and remote. 'Let's all sit down to supper.' She turned and left the room.

Joe stood defeated.

Ma said, 'Now there's a girl with spunk.'

He arose at midnight and searched the parlor.

The room was empty.

The radio was still on, warm. Faintly, inside it, like a tiny mosquito's voice, he heard someone, far away saying, 'Land sakes, land sakes, land sakes, land o' Goshen!'

The room was cold. He shivered. The radio was warm with his ear against it.

'Land sakes, land o' Goshen, land sakes—'

He cut it off.

His wife heard him sink into bed.

'She's gone,' he said.

'Of course,' she said. 'Until tomorrow at ten.'

He did not question this.

'Good night, baby,' he said.

The living room was filled only with sunlight at

breakfast. He laughed out loud to see the emptiness. He felt relief, like a good drink of wine, in himself. He whistled on his way to the office.

Ten o'clock was coffee time. Marching along the avenue, humming, he heard the radio playing in front of the electrical parts store.

'Shuffle,' said a voice. 'Lands, I wish you wouldn't track the house with your muddy shoes.'

He stopped. He pivoted like a wax figure, turning on its slow, cold axis, in the street.

He heard the voice.

'Ma Perkins's voice,' he whispered.

He listened.

'It's *her* voice,' he said. 'The woman who was at our house last night. I'm positive.'

And yet, late last night, the empty parlor?

But what about the radio, humming, warm, all alone in the room, and the faint faraway voice repeating and repeating, 'Land sakes, land sakes, land sakes . . .'?

He ran into a drugstore and dropped a nickel into the pay telephone slot.

Three buzzes. A short wait.

Click.

'Hello, Annie?' he said gaily.

'No, this is Ma,' said a voice.

'Oh,' he said.

He dropped the phone back onto its hook.

*   *   *

He didn't let himself think of it that afternoon. It was an impossible thing, a thing of some subtle and inferior horror. On his way home he purchased a bundle of fresh moist pink rosebuds for Anna. He had them in his right hand when he opened the door of his apartment. He had almost forgotten about Ma by then.

He dropped the rosebuds on the floor and did not stoop to retrieve them. He only stared and continued to stare at Ma, who was seated in that chair that did not rock, rocking.

Her sweet voice called cheerily. 'Evenin', Joe boy! Ain't you thoughtful, fetchin' home roses!'

Without a word he dialed a phone number.

'Hello, Ed? Say, Ed, you doing anything this evening?'

The answer was negative.

'Well, how about dropping up, then, I need your help, Ed.'

The answer was positive.

At eight o'clock they were finishing supper and Ma was clearing away the dishes. 'Now for dessert tomorrow,' she was saying, 'we'll have crisscross squash pie—'

The doorbell rang, and, answering, Joe Tiller almost hauled Ed Leiber out of his shoes. 'Take it easy, Joe,' said Ed, rubbing his hand.

'Ed,' said Joe, seating him with a small glass of sherry. 'You know my wife, and this is Ma Perkins.'

Ed laughed. 'How are you? Heard you on the radio for years!'

'It's no laughing matter, Ed,' said Joe. 'Cut it.'

'I didn't mean to be facetious, Mrs Perkins,' said Ed. 'It's just that your name is so similar to that fictional character—'

'Ed,' said Joe. 'This *is* Ma Perkins.'

'That's right,' said Ma charmingly, shelling some peas.

'You're all kidding me,' said Ed, looking around.

'No,' said Ma.

'She's come to stay and I can't get her out, Ed. Ed, you're a psychologist, what do I do? I want you to talk to Annie, here. It's all in her mind.'

Ed cleared his throat. 'This has gone far enough.' He walked over to touch Ma's hand. 'She's real, not a hallucination.' He touched Annie. 'Annie's real.' He touched Joe. '*You're* real. We're *all* real. How are things at work, Joe?'

'Don't change the subject, I'm serious. She's moved in and I want her moved out—'

'Well, that's for the OPA to decide, I guess, or the sheriff's office, not a psychologist—'

'Ed, listen to me, listen, Ed, I know it sounds crazy, but she really is the *original* Ma Perkins.'

'Let me smell your breath, Joe.'

'And I want her to stay on here with me,' said Annie. 'I get lonely days. I stay home and do the housework and I need company. I won't have her moved out. She's mine!'

Ed slapped his knee and exhaled. 'There you are, Joe.

Looks like you want a divorce lawyer instead of a psychologist.'

Joe swore. 'I can't go off and leave her here in this old witch's clutches, don't you understand? I love her too much. There's no telling *what* may happen to her if I leave her alone here for the next year without communicating with the outer world!'

'Keep your voice down, Joe, you're screaming. Now, now.' The psychologist turned his attention to the old woman. 'What do you say? *Are* you Ma Perkins?'

'I am. From the radio.'

The psychologist wilted. There was something in the direct, honest way she said it. He began to look for the door, his hands twitching on his knees.

'And I came here because Annie needs me,' said Ma. 'Why I know this child better and she knows me better than her own husband.'

The psychologist said, 'Aha. Just a minute. Come along, Joe.' They stepped out into the hall and whispered. 'Joe, I hate to tell you this, but they're both – not well. Who *is* she? Your mother-in-law?'

'I told you, she's Ma—'

'God damn it, cut it out, I'm your friend, Joe. We're not in the room with them. We humor them, yes, but not me.' He was irritable.

Joe exhaled. 'Okay, have it your way. But you do believe I'm in a mess, don't you?'

'I do. What's the deal, have they both been sitting at

home listening to the radio too much? That explains them both having the same idea at the same time.'

Joe was going to try to explain the whole thing, but gave up. Ed might think he was crazy, too. 'Will you help me? What can we do?'

'Leave that to me. I'll give them a little logic. Come on.'

They reentered, and refilled their glasses with sherry. Once comfortable again, Ed looked at the two ladies and said, 'Annie, this lady isn't Ma Perkins.'

'Oh, yes, she is,' said Annie angrily.

'No, because if she was I wouldn't be able to see her, only you could see her, do you understand?'

'No.'

'If she was Ma Perkins, I could make her disappear just by convincing you how illogical it is to think of her as real. I'd tell you she's nothing but a radio character made up by someone—'

'Young man,' said Ma. 'Life is life. One form's as good as another. I was born, maybe just in someone's head, but I'm born and kicking and getting more real every year that I live. You and you and you, every time you hear me, make me more real. Why, if I died tomorrow, everybody all over the country would cry, wouldn't they?'

'Well—'

'Wouldn't they?' she snapped.

'Yes, but only over an idea, not a real thing.'

'Over a thing they think is real. And thinkin' is bein', you young fool,' said Ma.

'It's no use,' said Ed. He turned once more to the wife. 'Look, Annie, this is your mother-in-law, her name really isn't Ma Perkins at all. It's your *mother-in-law*.' He pronounced each word clearly and heavily.

'That'd be nice,' agreed Annie. 'I like that.'

'I wouldn't object,' said Ma. 'Worse things have happened in my life.'

'Are we all agreed now?' said Ed, surprised at his sudden success. 'She's your mother-in-law, Annie?'

'Yes.'

'And you're not Ma Perkins at all, right, ma'am?'

'Is it a plot, a game, a secret?' said Annie, looking at Ma.

Ma smiled.

'If you want to put it that way, yes.'

'But look here,' objected Joe.

'Shut up, Joe, you'll spoil everything.' To the other two, 'Now, let's repeat it. She's your mother-in-law. Her name is Ma Tiller.'

'Ma Tiller,' said the two women.

'I want to see you outside,' said Joe, and lurched Ed out of the room. He held him against the wall and threatened him with a fist. 'You fool! I don't want her to stay on, I want to get rid of her. Now you've helped make Annie worse, made her believe in that old witch!'

'Worse, you nut, I've cured her, both of them. Fine appreciation!' And Ed struggled to get free. 'I'll send a bill over in the morning!' He stalked down the hall.

Joe hesitated a moment before entering the room again. Oh God, he thought. God help me.

'Hello,' said Ma, looking up, preparing a home-packed bottle of cucumber pickles.

At midnight and breakfast again, the living room was empty. Joe got a crafty glint in his eyes. He looked at the radio and stroked the top of it with his trembling hand.

'Stay away from there!' cried his wife.

'Oho,' he said. 'Is this where she hides at night, in here, eh? In here! This is her coffin, eh, this is where the damn old vampire sleeps until tomorrow when her sponsor lets her out!'

'Keep your hands off,' she said hysterically.

'Well, that settles her hash.' He picked the radio up in his hands. 'How do you kill her sort of witch? With a silver bullet through the heart? With a crucifix? With wolfsbane? Or do you make the sign of a cross on a soapbox top? Eh, is that it?'

'Give me that!' His wife rushed over to grapple with him. Between them, they swayed back and forth in a titanic battle for the electric coffin between them.

'There!' he shouted.

He flung the radio to the floor. He tromped and stomped on it. He kicked it into bits. He ravened at it. He held the tubes in his hands and smashed them into silver flinders. Then he stuffed the shattered entrails into the wastebasket, all the time his wife danced frantically about, sobbing and screaming.

'She's dead,' he said. 'Dead, God damn it! I've fixed her good.'

His wife cried herself to sleep. He tried to calm her, but she was so deep in her hysteria he could not touch her. Death was a terrible incident in her life.

In the morning, she spoke not a word. In the coolness of the separated house, he ate his breakfast, confident that things would be better by evening.

He arrived late to work. He walked between the typing, clicking rows of stenographers' desks, passed on down the long hallway, and opened the door of his secretary's office.

His secretary was standing against her desk, her face pale, her hands up to her lips. 'Oh, Mr Tiller, I'm so glad you came,' she said. 'In there.' She pointed at the door to the inner office. 'That awful old busybody! She just came in and – and—' She hurried to the door, flung it open. 'You'd better see her!'

He felt sick to his stomach. He shuffled across the threshold and shut the door. Then he turned to confront the old woman who was in his office.

'How did you get here?' he demanded.

'Why, good morning.' Ma Perkins laughed, peeling potatoes in his swivel chair, her tidy little black shoes twinkling in the sunlight. 'Come on in. I decided your business needed reorganizing. So I just started. We're partners now. I had lotsa experience in this line. I saved more failing businesses, more bad romances, more lives. You're just what I need.'

'Get out,' he said flatly, his mouth tight.

'Why now, young man, cheer up. We'll have your business turned around in no time. Just let an old woman philosophize and tell you how—'

'You heard what I said,' he grated. 'Isn't it enough I had trouble with you at my house?'

'Who, me?' She shook her head. 'Sakes, I never been to your house.'

'Liar!' he cried. 'You tried to break up our home!'

'I only been here in the office, for six months now,' she said.

'I never saw you here before.'

'Oh, I been around, around, I been observin'. I seed your business was bad, I thought I'd just give you some gumption you need.'

Then he realized how it was. There were two Mas. One here, one at home. Two? No, a million. A different one in every home. None aware of the others' separate lives. All different, as shaped by the individual brains of those who heard and lived in the far homes. 'I see,' he said. 'So you're takin' over, moving in on me, are you, you old bastard?'

'Sech language.' She chuckled, making a crisscross pie on his green blotter, rolling out the yellow dough with plump fingers.

'Who is it?' he snarled.

'Eh?'

'Who is it, who's the traitor in this office?!' he bellowed. 'The one who listens to you in secret here, on my time?'

'Ask me no questions, I'll tell you no fibs,' she said, pouring cinnamon out of his inkwell onto the piecrust dough.

'Just wait!' He rammed the door open and ran past his secretary and out into the big room. 'Attention!' He waved his arms. The typing stopped. The ten stenographers and clerks turned away from their shiny black machines. 'Listen,' he said. 'Is there a radio somewhere in this office?'

Silence.

'You heard what I said,' he demanded, glaring at them with hot eyes. 'Is there a radio?'

A trembling silence.

'I'll give a bonus and a guarantee I won't fire her, to anyone who tells me where the radio is!' he announced.

One of the little blond stenographers put up her hand.

'In the ladies' restroom,' she whimpered. 'Cigarette time, we play it low.'

'God bless you!'

In the hall, he pounced on the restroom door. 'Is anyone in there?' he called. Silence. He opened the door. He entered.

The radio was on the window ledge. He seized it, jerking

at its wires. He felt as if he were clutching at the live intestines of some horrible animal. He opened the window and flung it out. Somewhere there was a scream. The radio burst into bomb fragments on the roof below.

He slammed the window and went back to his office door.

The office was empty.

He picked up his inkwell and shook it until it gave forth—

Ink.

Driving home, he considered what he had said to the office force. Never another radio, he had said. Whoever is responsible for another radio will be fired out of hand. Fired, did they understand!

He walked up the flight of stairs and stopped.

A party was going on in his apartment. He heard his wife laughing, drinks being passed, music playing, voices.

'Oh, Ma, aren't you the one?'

'Pepper, where are you?'

'Out here, Dad!'

'Fluffy, let's play spin the bottle!'

'Henry, Henry Aldrich, put down that platter before you break it!'

'John, oh, John, John!'

'Helen, you look lovely—'

'And I said to Dr Trent—'

'I want you to meet Dr. Christian and—'

'Sam, Sam Spade, this is Philip Marlowe—'

'Hello, Marlowe.'

'Hello, Spade!'

Gushing laughter. Rioting. Tinkling glass.

Voices.

Joe fell against the wall. Warm perspiration rolled down his face. He put his hands to his throat and wanted to scream. Those voices. Familiar. Familiar. All familiar. Where had he heard them before? Friends of Annie's? And yet she had no friends. None. He could remember none of her few friends' voices. And these names, these strange familiar names—?

He swallowed drily. He put his hand to the door. *Click.*

The voices vanished. The music was cut off. The tinkling of glass ceased. The laughter faded in a great wind.

When he stepped through the door, it was like coming into a room an instant after a hurricane has left by the window. There was a sense of loss, a vacuum, an emptiness, a vast silence. The walls ached.

Annie sat looking at him.

'Where did they go?' he said.

'Who?' She tried to look surprised.

'Your friends,' he said.

'What friends?' She raised her eyebrows.

'You know what I'm talking about,' he said.

'No,' she said firmly.

'What'd you do? Go buy a new radio?'

'And what if I did?'

He took a step forward, his hands groping the air. 'Where is it?'

'I won't tell.'

'I'll find it,' he said.

'I'll only buy another and another,' she said.

'Annie, Annie,' he said, stopping. 'How long are you going to carry this crazy thing on? Don't you see what's happening?'

She looked at the wall. 'All I know is that you've been a bad husband, neglecting me, ignoring me. You're gone, and when you're gone, I have my friends, and my friends and I have parties and I watch them live and die and walk around, and we drink drinks and have affairs, oh yes, you wouldn't believe it, have affairs, my dear Joseph! And we have martinis and daiquiris and manhattans, my good Joseph! And we sit and talk and crochet or cook or even take trips to Bermuda or anywhere at all, Rio, Martinique, Paris! And now, tonight, we had such a grand party, until you came to haunt us!'

'Haunt you!' he shrieked, eyes wild.

'Yes,' she whispered. 'It's almost as if you're not real at all. As if you're some phantom from another world come to spoil our fun. Oh, Joseph, why don't you go away.'

He said slowly, 'You're insane. God help you, Annie, but you're insane.'

'Whether I am or not,' she said, at last, 'I've come to a decision. I'm leaving you, tonight. I'm going home to Mother!'

He laughed wearily. 'You haven't got a mother. She's dead.'

'I'm going anyway, home to Mother,' she said endlessly.

'Where's that radio?' he said.

'No,' she said. 'I wouldn't be able to go home if you took it. You can't have it.'

'Damn it!'

Someone knocked on the door.

He went to answer it. The landlord was there. 'You'll have to stop shouting,' he said. 'The neighbors are complaining.'

'I'm sorry,' said Joe, stepping outside and half-shutting the door. 'We'll try to be quiet—'

Then he heard the running feet. Before he could turn, the door slammed and locked. He heard Annie cry out triumphantly. He hammered at the door. 'Annie, let me in, you fool!'

'Now, take it easy, Mr Tiller,' cautioned the landlord.

'That little idiot in there, I've got to get inside—'

He heard the voices again, the loud and the high voices, and the shrill wind blowing and the dancing music and the glasses tinkling. And a voice saying, 'Let him in, let him do whatever he wants. We'll fix him. So he'll never hurt us again.'

He kicked at the door.

'Stop that,' said the landlord. 'I'll call the police.'

'Call them, then!'

The landlord ran to find a phone.

Joe broke the door down.

Annie was sitting on the far side of the room. The room was dark, only the light from a little ten-dollar radio illuminating it. There were a lot of people there, or maybe shadows. And in the center of the room, in the rocking chair, was the old woman.

'Why, look who's here,' she said, enchanted.

He walked forward and put his fingers around her neck.

Ma Perkins tried to get free, screamed, thrashed, but could not.

He strangled her.

When he was done with her, he let her drop to the floor, the paring knife, the spilled peas flung everywhere. She was cold. Her heart was stopped. She was dead.

'That's just what we wanted you to do,' said Annie tonelessly, sitting in the dark.

'Turn the lights on,' he gasped, reeling. He staggered back across the room. What was it, anyway? A plot? Were they going to enter other rooms, all around the world? Was Ma Perkins dead, or just dead here? Was she alive everywhere else?

The police were coming in the door, the landlord behind them. They had guns. 'All right, buddy, up with them!'

They bent over the lifeless body on the floor.

Annie was smiling. 'I saw it all,' she said. 'He killed her.'

'She's dead all right,' said one of the policemen.

'She's not real, she's not real,' sobbed Joe. 'She's not real, believe me.'

'She feels real to me,' said the cop. 'Dead as hell.'

Annie smiled.

'She's not real, listen to me, she's Ma Perkins!'

'Yeah, and I'm Charlie's aunt. Come on along, fellow!'

He felt himself turn and then it came to him, in one horrid rush, what it would be like from here on. After tonight, him taken away, and Annie returned home, to her radio, alone in her room for the next thirty years. And all the little lonely people and the other people, the couples, and groups all over the country in the next thirty years, listening and listening. And the lights changing to mists and the mists to shadows and the shadows to voices and the voices to shapes and the shapes to realities, until, at last, as here, all over the country, there would be rooms, with people in them, some real, some not, some controlled by unrealities, until all was a nightmare, one not knowable from the other. Ten million rooms with ten million old women named Ma peeling potatoes in them, chuckling, philosophizing. Ten million rooms in which some boy named Aldrich played with marbles on the floor. Ten million rooms where guns barked and ambulances rumbled. God, God, what a huge, engulfing plot. The world was lost, and he had lost it for them. It had been lost before he began. How many other husbands are starting the same fight tonight, doomed to lose at last, as he lost, because the rules of logic have been warped all out of shape by a little black evil electric box?

He felt the police snap the silver handcuffs tight.

Annie was smiling. And Annie would be here, night after night, with her wild parties and her laughter and travels, while he was far away.

'Listen to me!' he screamed.

'You're nuts!' said the cop, and hit him.

On the way down the hall, a radio was playing.

In the warm light of the room as they passed the door, Joe peered swiftly in, one instant. There, by the radio, rocking, was an old woman, shelling some fresh green peas.

He heard a door slam far away and his feet drifted.

He stared at the hideous old woman, or was it a man, who occupied the chair in the center of the warm and swept-clean living room. What was she doing? Knitting, shaving herself, peeling potatoes? Shelling peas? Was she sixty, eighty, one hundred, ten million years old?

He felt his jaw clench and his tongue lie cold and remote in his mouth.

'Come in,' said the old woman–old man. 'Annie's fixing dinner in the kitchen.'

'Who are you?' he asked, his heart trembling.

'You know me,' the person said, laughing shrilly. 'I'm Ma Perkins. You know, you know, you know.'

In the kitchen he held to the wall and his wife turned toward him with a cheese grater in her hand. 'Darling!'

'Who's – who's—' He felt drunk, his tongue thick. 'Who's that person in the living room, how did she get here?'

'Why, it's only Ma Perkins, you know, from the radio,' his wife said with casual logic. She kissed him a sweet kiss on the mouth. 'Are you cold? You're shaking.'

He had time only to see her nod a smile before they dragged him on.

Doubles

Bernard Trimble played tennis against his wife and when he beat her she was unhappy and when she beat him he was demon-possessed and double-damn madness unhappy, to put it mildly.

One summer, on a country road, in verdant Santa Barbara, Bernard Trimble was motoring along a farm-land road with a beautiful and compatible lady of recent acquaintance in the seat beside him, her hair whipping in the wind, with her bright scarf snapping, and a look of philosophic tiredness on her face as from recent pleasant exertions, when an open roadster gunned past them going in the opposite direction, with a woman driving and a young man lounging beside her.

'My God!' cried Trimble.

'Why'd you just cry "my God"?' said the beautiful temptress at his side.

'My wife just passed with the most terrible look on her face.'

'What kind of look?'

'Just like the one you have right now,' said Trimble.

And he gunned the car down the road.

At an early dinner that night at the tennis club, with the sound of the tennis balls flying back and forth like soft doves, Trimble sat between two lit candles heartily devouring a bottle of wine. He growled when his wife finally arrived after much too long a shower and sat across from him wearing a spider-woven Spanish mantilla and a phosphorescent breath, like the breath of a twilight forest, sighing from her mouth.

He bent close to examine her chin, her cheeks, and her eyes.

'No, it's not there.'

'What's not there?' she asked.

The look, he thought, of remembered and pleasant exertion.

She in turn bent forward, searching his face.

He leaned back in his chair and at last got the courage to say, 'A strange thing happened this afternoon.'

His wife took a sip of wine and replied, 'Strange, I was going to say somewhat the same thing.'

'You first, then,' he said.

'No, go ahead. Tell me the strange thing.'

'Well,' he said. 'I was driving along a country road outside town when a car passed, going the other way. There was a woman in it who looked very much like you. In the seat beside her, wearing an extravagantly rich white suit, his hair whipping in the wind and looking terribly and pleasantly tired, was the billionaire tennis-playing magnate Charles William Bishop. It was all over in a second and the car was gone. After all, we were traveling forty miles an hour.'

'Eighty,' said his wife. 'Two cars passing each other in opposite directions at forty miles an hour, the aggregate is eighty.'

'Oh yes,' he agreed. 'Well, wasn't that strange?'

'Indeed,' said his wife. 'Now let me tell you my strangeness. I was driving in a car this afternoon on a country road and a car passed at an accumulated eighty miles an hour and I thought I saw a man in it who looked very much like you. In the seat beside him was that beautiful heiress from Spain, Carlotta de Vega Montenegro. It was all over in a second and I was stunned and drove on. Two strange occurrences, yes?'

'Have some more wine,' he said quietly. He filled her glass much too full and they sat for a long while studying each other's face and drinking the wine.

They listened to the soft sound of the dovelike tennis balls being struck and tossed through the twilight air;

there seemed to be a lot of people out on the courts, enjoying themselves.

He cleared his throat and at last picked up a knife and began to run its edge along the tablecloth between them.

'I think,' he said, 'this is the way we solve our two strange problems.'

With his knife he scored a long rectangle in the cloth and cut across it so that it resembled a metaphorical tennis court on the table.

Trimble and his wife looked across the net at the figures of Charles William Bishop and Carlotta de Vega Montenegro walking away, shaking their heads, their shoulders slumped in the noonday sun.

His wife lifted a towel to touch his cheek and he lifted one to touch hers.

'Well done!' he said.

'Bull's-eye!' she said.

And they looked into each other's face to find a look of tired contentment from recent amiable exertions.

Pater Caninus

Young Father Kelly edged his way into Father Gilman's office, stopped, turned, and looked as if he might go back out, and then turned back again.

Father Gilman looked up from his papers and said, 'Father Kelly, is there a problem?'

'I'm not quite sure,' said Father Kelly.

Father Gilman said, 'Well, are you coming or going? Please, come in, and sit.'

Father Kelly slowly inched back in and at last sat and looked at the older man.

'Well?' said Father Gilman.

'Well,' said Father Kelly. 'This is all very silly and very strange, and maybe I shouldn't bring it up at all.'

Here he stopped. Father Gilman waited.

'It has to do with that dog, Father.'

'What dog?'

'You know, the one here in the hospital. Every Tuesday and Thursday there's that dog with the red bandanna that makes the rounds with Father Riordan, patrolling the first and second floors – around, up, down, in and out. The patients love that dog. It makes them happy.'

'Ah, yes, I know the dog you mean,' said Father Gilman. 'What a gift it is to have animals like that in the hospital. But what is troubling you about this particular dog?'

'Well,' said Father Kelly. 'Do you have a few minutes to come watch that dog, because he's doing something very peculiar right now.'

'Peculiar? How?'

'Well, Father,' said Father Kelly, 'the dog has come back to the hospital twice this week already – on his own – and he's here again now.'

'Father Riordan isn't with him?'

'No, Father. That's what I'm trying to get at. The dog is making his rounds, all on his own, without Father Riordan telling him where to go.'

Father Gilman chuckled. 'Is that all? Clearly, he's just a very smart dog. Like the horse that used to pull the milk wagon when I was a boy – it knew exactly which houses to stop and wait at without the milkman saying a word.'

'No, no. He's up to something. But, I'm not sure what, so I want you to come see for yourself.'

Sighing, Father Gilman rose and said, 'All right, let's go look at this most peculiar beast.'

'This way, Father,' said Father Kelly, and led him out into the hall and up the stairs to the second floor.

'I think he's somewhere here now, Father,' said Father Kelly. 'Ah, there.'

At which moment the dog with the red bandanna trotted out of room 17 and moved on, without looking at them, into room 18.

They stood outside the door and watched the dog who was sitting by the bed and seemed to be waiting.

The patient in the bed began to speak, and as Father Gilman and Father Kelly listened, they heard the man whispering while the dog sat there patiently.

Finally, the whispering stopped and the dog reached out a paw, touched the bed, waited a moment, and then came trotting out to move on to the next room.

Father Kelly looked at Father Gilman. 'How does that strike you? What was he doing?'

'Good Lord,' said Father Gilman. 'I think the dog was—'

'What, Father?'

'I think the dog was taking confession.'

'It can't be.'

'Yes. Can't be, but *is*.'

The two priests stood there in the semidarkness, listening to the voice of another patient whispering. They moved toward the door and looked in the room. The dog sat there quietly as the penitent unburdened his soul.

Finally they saw the dog reach out its paw to touch the bed, then turn and trot out of the room, hardly noticing them.

The two priests stood, riveted, and then silently followed.

At the next room the dog went to sit beside the bed. After a moment the patient saw the dog and smiled and said in a faint voice, 'Oh, bless me.'

The dog sat quietly as the patient began to whisper.

They followed the dog along the hall, from room to room.

Along the way the young priest looked at the older one and noticed that Father Gilman's face was beginning to contort and grow very red indeed, until the veins stood out on his brow.

Finally the dog finished its rounds and started down the stairs.

The two priests followed.

When they got to the hospital doors, the dog was starting out into the twilight; there was no one there to greet it or lead it away.

At which moment Father Gilman suddenly exploded and cried out: 'You! You there! Dog! Don't come back, you hear?! Come back and I'll call damnation, hell, brimstone, and fire down on your head. You hear me, dog?! Go on, get out, go!'

The dog, startled, spun in a circle and bounded away.

The old priest stood there, his breathing heavy, eyes shut, and his face crimson.

Young Father Kelly gazed off into the dark.

Finally he gasped, 'Father, what have you done?!'

'Damnation,' said the older priest. 'That sinful, terrible, horrible beast!'

'Horrible, Father?' said Father Kelly. 'Didn't you hear what was said?'

'I heard,' said Father Gilman. 'Taking it on himself to forgive, to offer penance, to hear the pleas of those poor patients!'

'But, Father,' cried Father Kelly. 'Isn't that what *we* do?'

'And that's our business,' gasped Father Gilman. 'Our business alone.'

'Is that true, Father? Aren't others like us?' said Father Kelly. 'I mean, in a good marriage, isn't pillow talk in the middle of the night a kind of confession? Isn't that the way young couples forgive and go on? Isn't that somehow like us?'

'Pillow talk!' cried Father Gilman. 'Pillow talk and dogs and sinful beasts!'

'Father, he may not come back!'

'Good riddance. I'll not have such things in my hospital!'

'My God, sir, didn't you see? He's a golden retriever. What a name. After an hour of listening to your penitents, to ask and forgive, wouldn't you love to hear me call you that?'

'Golden retriever?'

'Yes. Think about it, Father,' said the young priest.
'Enough. Come. Let's go back and see if that beast, as
you call him, has done any harm.'

Father Kelly went back into the hospital. Moments
later, the older priest followed. They walked along
the hall and looked in the rooms at the patients in
their beds. A peculiar sound of silence hung over the
place.

In one room they saw a look of strange peace.

In another room they heard whispering. Father Gilman
thought he caught the name Mary, though he could not
be sure.

And so they roamed among the quiet rooms on this
special night and as the older priest walked along he felt
his skins fall away – a skin of ignorance, a layer of
contempt, and then a subdermis of neglect – so that
when he arrived back at his office he felt as if he had
shed an invisible flesh.

Father Kelly said good night and left.

The old priest sat and covered his eyes, leaning against
the desk.

After a few moments of silence, he heard a sound and
looked up.

In the doorway the dog stood, waiting there quietly;
it had come back on its own. The dog hardly breathed
and did not whimper or bark or sigh. It came forward,
very quietly, and sat across the desk from the priest.

The priest looked into that golden face and the dog looked back.

Finally the old priest said, 'Bless me, what do I call you? I can think of nothing. But bless me, please, for I have sinned.'

The priest then spoke of his arrogance and the sin of pride and all the other sins he had committed that day.

And the dog, sitting there, listened.

Arrival and Departure

No day in all of time began with nobler heart or fresher spirit. No morn had ever chanced upon its greener self as did this morn discover spring in every aspect and every breath. Birds flew about, intoxicated, and moles and all things holed up in earth and stone ventured forth, forgetting that life itself might be forfeit. The sky was a Pacific, a Caribbean, an Indian sea, hung in a tidal outpouring over a town that now exhaled the dust of winter from a thousand windows. Doors slammed wide. Like a tide moving over a town that now exhaled the dust of winter from a thousand windows. Doors slammed wide. Like a tide moving into a shore, wave after wave of laundered curtains broke over the piano-wire lines behind the houses.

And at last the mild sweetness of this particular day

summoned forth two souls, like wintry figures from a Swiss clock, hypnotized, upon their porch. Mr and Mrs Alexander, twenty-four months locked deep in their rusty house, felt long-forgotten wings stir in their shoulder blades as the sun rekindled their bones.

'Smell *that*!'

Mrs Alexander took a drink of air and spun to accuse the house. 'Two years! One hundred sixty-five bottles of throat molasses! Ten pounds of sulfur! Twelve boxes of sleeping pills! Five yards of flannel for our chests! How much mustard grease? Get away!' She pushed at the house. She turned to the spring day, opened her arms. The sun made teardrops jump from her eyes.

They waited, not yet ready to descend away from two years of nursing each other, falling ill time and again, accepting but never quite enjoying the prospect of another evening together after six hundred of seeing no other human face.

'Why, we're strangers here.' The husband nodded to the shady streets.

And they remembered how they had stopped answering the door and kept the shades down, afraid that some abrupt encounter, some flash of bright sun, might shatter them to dusty ghosts.

But now, on this fountain-sparkling day, their health at last miraculously returned, old Mr and Mrs Alexander edged down the steps and into the town, like tourists from a land beneath the earth.

Reaching the main street, Mr Alexander said, 'We're not so old; we just *felt* old. Why I'm seventy-two, you're only seventy. I'm out for some special shopping, Elma. Meet you here in two hours!'

They flew apart, rid of each other at last.

Not half a block away, passing a dress shop, Mr Alexander saw a mannequin in a window, and froze. There, ah, there! The sunlight warmed her pink cheeks, her berry-stained lips, her blue-lacquer eyes, her yellow-yarn hair. He stood at the window for an entire minute, until a live woman appeared suddenly, arranging the displays. When she glanced up, there was Mr Alexander, smiling like a youthful idiot. She smiled back.

What a day! he thought. I could punch a hole in a plank door. I could throw a cat over the courthouse! Get out of the way, old man! Wait! Was that a *mirror*? Never mind. Good God! I'm really alive!

Mr Alexander was inside the shop.

'I want to buy something!' he said.

'What?' asked the beautiful saleslady.

He glanced foolishly about. 'Why, let me have a scarf. That's it, a scarf.'

He blinked at the numerous scarves she brought, smiling at him so his heart roared and tilted like a gyro-scope, throwing the world out of balance. 'Pick the scarf you'd wear, yourself. That's the scarf for me.'

She chose a scarf the color of her eyes.

'Is it for your wife?'

He handed her a five-dollar bill. 'Put the scarf on.' She obeyed. He tried to imagine Elma's head sticking out above it; failed. 'Keep it,' he said. 'It's yours.' He drifted out the sunlit door, his veins singing.

'Sir,' she called, but he was gone.

What Mrs Alexander wanted most was shoes, and after leaving her husband she entered the very first shoe shop. But not, however, before she dropped a penny in a perfume machine and pumped great vaporous founts of verbena upon her sparrow chest. Then, with the spray clinging round her like morning mist, she plunged into the shoe store, where a fine young man with doe-brown eyes and black arched brows and hair with the sheen of patent leather pinched her ankles, feathered her instep, caressed her toes, and so entertained her feet that they blushed a soft, warm pink.

'Madame has the smallest foot I've fitted this year. Extraordinarily small.'

Mrs Alexander was a great heart seated there, beating so loudly that the salesman had to shout over the sound:

'If Madame will push down!'

'Would the lady like another color?'

He shook her left hand as she departed with three pairs of shoes, giving her fingers what seemed to be a meaningful appraisal. She laughed a strange laugh, forgetting to say she had not worn her wedding band, her fingers had puffed with illness so many years that the ring now lay in dust. On the street, she confronted the verbena-squirting machine, another copper penny in her hand.

Mr Alexander strode with great bouncing strides up and down streets, doing a little jig of delight on meeting certain people, stopping at last, faintly tired, but not admitting it to anyone, before the United Cigar store. There, as if seven-hundred-odd noons had not vanished, stood Mr Bleak, Mr Grey, Samuel Spaulding, and the Wooden Indian. They seized and punched Mr Alexander in disbelief.

'John, you're back from the dead!'

'Coming to the lodge tonight?'

'Sure!'

'Oddfellows meeting tomorrow night?'

'I'll be there!' Invitations blew about him in a warm wind. 'Old friends, I've *missed* you!' He wanted to grab everyone, even the Indian. They lit his free cigar and bought him foamy beers next door in the jungle color of green-felt pool tables.

'One week from tonight,' cried Mr Alexander. 'Open house. My wife and I invite you all, good friends. Barbecue! Drinks and fun!'

Spaulding crushed his hand. 'Will your wife mind about tonight?'

'Not Elma.'

'I'll come for you at eight o'clock.'

'Fine!'

And Mr Alexander was off like a ball of Spanish moss blown on the wind.

After she left the store, Mrs Alexander was discovered in the streets of the town by a sea of women. She was the center of a bargain sale, ladies clustering in twos and threes, everyone talking, laughing, offering, accepting at once.

'Tonight, Elma. The Thimble Club.'

'Come pick me up!'

Breathless and flushed, she pushed through, made it to a far curb, looked back as one looks at the ocean for a last time before going inland, and hustled, lighting to herself, down the avenue, counting on her fingers the appointments she had in the next week at the Elm Street Society, the Women's Patriotic League, the Sewing Basket, and the Elite Theatre Club.

The hours blazed to their finish. The courthouse clock rang once.

Mr Alexander stood on the street corner, glancing at his watch doubtfully and shaking it, muttering under his breath. A woman was standing on the opposite corner, and after ten minutes of waiting, Mr Alexander crossed over. 'I beg your pardon, but I think my watch is wrong,' he called, approaching. 'Could you give me the correct time?'

'John!' she cried.

'Elma!' he cried.

'I was standing here all the time,' she said.

'And *I* was standing over there!'

'You've got a new suit!'

'That's a new dress!'

'New hat.'

'So is yours.'

'New shoes.'

'How do *yours* fit?'

'Mine hurt.'

'So do mine.'

'I bought tickets for a play Saturday night for us, Elma! And made reservations for the Green Town picnic next month! What's that perfume you're wearing?'

'What's that cologne *you've* got on?'

'No *wonder* we didn't recognize each other!'

They looked at each other for a long time.

'Well, let's get home. Isn't it a beautiful day?'

They squeaked along in their new shoes. 'Yes, beautiful!' they both agreed, smiling. But then they glanced at each other out of the corner of their eyes and suddenly looked away, nervously.

Their house was blue dark; it was like entering a cave after the fresh green spring afternoon.

'How about a little lunch?'

'Not hungry. You?'

'Me neither.'

'I sure do like my new shoes.'

'Mine, too.'

'Well, what'll we do the rest of the day?'

'Oh, go to a show, maybe.'

'After we rest awhile.'

'You're not *tired*!'

'No, no, no,' she cried hastily. *'You?'*

'No, no!' he said quickly.

They sat down and felt the comfortable darkness and coolness of the room after the bright, glaring warm day.

'I think I'll just loosen my shoelaces a bit,' he said. 'Just untie the knots a moment.'

'I think I'll do the same.'

They loosened the knots and the laces in their shoes.

'Might as well get our hats off!'

Sitting there, they removed their hats.

He looked over at her and thought: Forty-five years. Married to her forty-five years. Why, I can remember . . . and that time in Mills Valley . . . and then there was that other day . . . forty years ago we drove to . . . yes . . . yes. His head shook. A long time.

'Why don't you take off your tie?' she suggested.

'Think I should, if we're going right out again?' he said.

'Just for a moment.'

She watched him take off his tie and she thought: It's been a good marriage. We've helped each other; he's spoon-fed, washed, and dressed me when I was sick, taken good care . . . Forty-five years now, and the honeymoon in Mills Valley – seems like only the day before the day before yesterday.

'Why don't you get rid of your earrings?' he suggested. 'New, aren't they? They look heavy.'

'They *are* a bit.' She laid them aside.

They sat in their comfortable soft chairs by the green baize tables where stood arnica bottles, pellet and tablet boxes, serums, cough remedies, pads, braces and foot rubs, greases, salves, lotions, inhalants, aspirin, quinine, powders, decks of worn playing cards from a million slow games of blackjack, and books they had murmured to each other across the dark small room in the single faint bulb light, their voices like the motion of dim moths through the shadows.

'Perhaps I can slip my shoes *off,*' he said. 'For one hundred and twenty seconds, before we run out again.'

'Isn't right to keep your feet boxed up all the time.'

They both slipped off their shoes.

'Elma?'

'Yes?' She looked up.

'Nothing,' he said.

They heard the mantel clock ticking. They caught each other peering at the clock. Two in the afternoon. Only six hours until eight tonight.

'John?' she said.

'Yes?'

'Never mind,' she said.

They sat.

'Why don't we put on our woolly slippers?' he wondered.

'I'll get them.'

She fetched the slippers.

They put them on, exhaling at the cool feel of the material.

'Ahhhhhh!'

'Why are you still wearing your coat and vest?'

'You know, new clothes *are* like a suit of armor.' He worked out of the coat and, a minute later, the vest.

The chairs creaked.

'Why, it's four o'clock,' she said, later.

'Time flies. Too late to go out now, isn't it?'

'Much too late. We'll just rest awhile. We can call a taxi to take us to supper.'

'Elma.' He licked his lips.

'Yes?'

'Oh, I forgot.' He glanced away at the wall.

'Why don't I just get out of my clothes into my bathrobe?' he suggested, five minutes later. 'I can dress in a rush when we stroll off for a big filet supper on the town.'

'Now you're being sensible,' she agreed. 'John?'

'Something you want to tell me?'

She gazed at the new shoes lying on the floor. She remembered the friendly tweak on her instep, the slow caress on her toes.

'No,' she said.

They listened for each other's hearts beating in the room. Clothed in their bathrobes, they sat sighing.

'I'm just the *least bit* tired. Not too much, understand,' she said. 'Just a *little bit*.'

'Naturally. It's been quite a day, quite a day.'

'You can't just *rush* out, can you?'

'Got to take it easy. We're not young anymore.'

'That's right.'

'I'm slightly exhausted, too,' he admitted casually.

'Maybe.' She glanced at the clock. 'Maybe we should have a bite *here* tonight. We can always dine out tomorrow evening.'

'A really smart suggestion,' he said. 'I'm not ravenous, anyway.'

'Strange, neither am I.'

'But, we'll go to a picture later tonight?'

'Of *course*!'

They sat munching cheese and some stale crackers like mice in the dark.

Seven o'clock.

'Do you know,' he said, 'I'm beginning to feel just a trifle queasy?'

'Oh?'

'Back aches.'

'Why don't I just rub it for you?'

'Thanks. Elma, you've got fine hands. You understand how to massage; not hard, not soft – but just *right*.'

'My feet are burning,' she said. 'I don't think I'll be able to make that film tonight.'

'Some other night,' he said.

'I wonder if something was wrong with that cheese? Heartburn.'

'Did *you* notice, too?'

They looked at the bottles on the table.

Seven-thirty. Seven forty-five.

'Almost eight o'clock.'

'John!' 'Elma!'

They had both spoken at once.

They laughed, startled.

'What is it?'

'You go ahead.'

'No, you first!'

They fell silent, listening and watching the clock, their hearts beating fast and faster. Their faces were pale.

'I think I'll take a little peppermint oil for my stomach,' said Mr Alexander.

'Hand me the spoon when you're done,' she said.

They sat smacking their lips in the dark, with only the one small moth-bulb lit.

Tickety-tickety-tick-tick-tick.

They heard the footsteps on their sidewalk. Up the front-porch stairs. The bell ringing.

They both stiffened.

The bell rang again.

They sat in the dark.

Six more times the bell rang.

'Let's not answer,' they both said. Startled again, they looked at each other, gasping.

They stared across the room into each other's eyes.

'It can't be anyone important.'

'No one important. They'd want to talk. And we're tired, aren't we?'

'Pretty,' she said.

The bell rang.

There was a tinkle as Mr Alexander took another spoonful of peppermint syrup. His wife drank some water and swallowed a white pill.

The bell rang a final, hard time.

'I'll just peek,' he said, 'out the front window.'

He left his wife and went to look. And there, on the front porch, his back turned, going down the steps, was Samuel Spaulding. Mr Alexander couldn't remember his face.

Mrs Alexander was in the other front room, looking out a window, secretly. She saw a Thimble Club woman walking along the street now, turning in at the sidewalk, coming up just as the man who had rung the bell was coming down. They met. Their voices murmured out there in the calm spring night.

The two strangers glanced up at the dark house together, discussing it.

Suddenly the two strangers laughed.

They gazed at the dim house once more. Then the

man and the woman walked down the sidewalk and away together, along the street, under the moonlit trees, laughing and shaking their heads and talking until they were out of sight.

Back in the living room, Mr Alexander found his wife had put out a small washtub of warm water in which, mutually, they might soak their feet. She had also brought in an extra bottle of arnica. He heard her washing her hands. When she returned from the bath, her hands and face smelled of soap instead of spring verbena.

They sat soaking their feet.

'I think we better turn in those tickets we bought for that play Saturday night,' he said, 'and the tickets for that benefit next week. You never can tell.'

'All right,' she said.

The spring afternoon seemed like a million years ago.

'I wonder who that was at the door,' she said.

'I don't know,' he said, reaching for the peppermint oil. He swallowed some. 'Game of blackjack, missus?'

She settled back in her chair with the faintest wriggle of her body.

'Don't mind if I do,' she said.

Last Laughs

His name was Andrew Rudolph Gerald Vesalius and he was a genius of the world, dialectician, statistician, creator of Italian operas, lyricist, poet of German lieder, Vedanta Temple lecturer, intellectual Santa Barbara brainstormer, and a grand pal.

This last seems unbelievable, for when we first met I was running on empty, a drab writer of pulp science fiction, earning two cents a word.

But Gerald, if I dare use his familiar name, discovered me and warned people that I had the future's eye and should be watched.

He coached me and let me travel as lapdog when he addressed relatives of Einstein, Jung, and Freud.

For years I transcribed his lectures, sat for tea with

Aldous Huxley, and trod speechless through art-gallery shows with Christopher Isherwood.

Now, suddenly, Vesalius was gone.

Well, almost. There were rumors that he was scribbling a book on those flying saucers that had hovered over the Palomar hot-dog stand and vanished.

I found that he no longer lectured at the Vedanta Temple, but survived in Paris or Rome; a promised novel was long overdue.

I telephoned his Malibu home ten dozen times.

Finally his secretary, William Hopkins Blair, admitted that Gerald was stricken with some mysterious disease.

I asked permission to visit my saintly friend. Blair disconnected.

I called again and Blair cried, in staccato phrases, that Vesalius had canceled our friendship.

Stunned, I tried to imagine how to apologize for sins which I knew I had not committed.

Then one evening at midnight the phone rang. A voice gasped one word: 'Help!'

'What?' I said.

The cry was repeated: 'Help!'

'Vesalius?' I cried.

A long silence.

'That sounds like you. Gerald?'

Silence, voices muttering, and then *buzzzz*.

I clenched the phone and felt a rush of tears come to my eyes; that *was* Vesalius's voice. After weeks of silent absence, he had cried out to me, implying some danger beyond my understanding.

The next evening, on impulse, I wandered around the Italian-named streets of upper Malibu and finally stopped at Vesalius's house.

I rang the bell.

No answer.

I rang again.

The house was silent.

I had spent twenty minutes ringing the bell and knocking when suddenly the door opened. That curious person, Gerald's keeper Blair, stood there staring at me.

'Yes?'

'After half an hour,' I said, 'all you have to say is *yes*?'

'Are you that pulp-writer friend of Gerald's?' he said.

'You know it,' I said. 'And I'm not just a pulp writer. I've come to see Gerald.'

Blair answered quickly. 'He's not here, he's in Rapallo.'

'I know he's here,' I lied. 'He called last night.'

'Impossible! He's in Italy!'

'No,' I lied again. 'He asked me to find a new doctor.'

Blair turned very pale.

'He's here,' I said. 'I know his voice.'

I stared down the hall, beyond Blair.

Suddenly he stood aside.

'Make it quick,' he said.

I ran along the hall to the bedroom and entered.

There, stretched out like a thin white marble carving on a sarcophagus lid, lay my old friend Vesalius.

'Gerald!' I cried.

The pale figure, looking ancient and stricken, remained silent, but the eyeballs revolved frantically in the thin face.

Blair, behind me, said, 'You see, he does poorly. Speak your piece and leave.'

I moved forward.

'What's wrong, Gerald?' I said. 'How can I help?'

There was a staccato pulse around Gerald's thin lips, but no answer, only a gray moth-flick of the eyeballs, glancing from me to Blair, and back again to me, frantically.

I panicked and thought to seize Gerald and flee, but there was no way.

I leaned over my friend and whispered in his ear. 'I'll be back,' I said. 'I promise, Gerald. I'll be back.'

I turned and hurried out of the room. At the front door Blair, staring beyond me, said: 'No, no more visitors. Vesalius prefers it.'

And the door shut.

I stood a long while wanting to ring and knock, knock and ring, but finally turned away.

I waited in the street for an hour; I could not bear to leave.

At one in the morning, all the house's lights went dark.

I crept around the side of the house toward the back

and found the French doors leading into Gerald's room open to the fresh night air.

Gerald Vesalius was as I had left him, eyes shut.

I cried softly, 'Gerald,' and his eyes flew wide open.

He was winter pale as before and stiff rigid, but his eyes jerked frantically.

I crept into the room and bent over the bed and whispered, 'Gerald, what's wrong?'

He could find no strength to answer, but at last he gasped and I thought I heard him say, 'Soli,' and then, 'tary,' and then 'confine,' and, gasp, 'ment!'

I put the syllables together, shocked.

'But why, Gerald?' I cried, as quietly as possible. 'Why?'

He could only jerk his chin toward the foot of his bed.

I pulled back the covers and stared.

His feet had been tied with adhesive tape to the end of the bed.

'So,' he gasped, 'couldn't,' he said, 'telephone!'

There was a phone to his right, just out of reach.

I unwound the adhesive and then bent back to question him.

'Can you hear me?'

His head jerked. He cried softly. 'Yes. Blair,' gasped, 'wants to,' he said, 'marry,' he gasped again, 'the . . . ancient . . . priest.' Then, in an ardent burst of words: 'Philosopher of all philosophers!'

'How's that again?'

'Marry,' the old man exploded, 'me!'

'Wait!' I was stunned. 'Marry?'

A frantic nod then, suddenly, a wild shriek of laughter.

'Me,' whispered Gerald Vesalius. 'Him.'

'Jesus! Blair and you? Wedding?'

'That's it.' Gerald's voice was clearer, stronger. 'That's it.'

'Impossible!'

'It is, it is!'

I felt a terrible urge toward laughter, but stopped.

'You mean—' I cried.

'Softly,' said Gerald, his voice fluid now. 'He'll hear, he'll throw,' he gasped, 'you out!'

'Gerald, that's not legal,' I cried softly.

'Legal,' he whispered, swallowed hard. 'Make legal, headlines, news!'

'My God!'

'Yes, God!'

'But why?'

'Doesn't,' said Gerald, 'care. Fame! Figures the more he wants to marry me, more fame and the more I will give him.'

'But again, why, Gerald?'

'He wants to own me, completely. Just,' said Gerald, 'in,' he said, 'his,' he gasped, 'nature.'

'Lord!' I said. 'I know marriages where a man owns the woman, or the woman completely owns the man.'

'Yes,' said Gerald. 'He wants that! He loves, but this is madness.'

Gerald stiffened, eyes shut, and then in a frail voice which rose and faded: 'Wants to own my mind.'

'He can't!'

'Will try, will try. Wants to be world's greatest philosopher.'

'Lunatic!'

'Yes! Wants to write, travel, lecture, wants to be me. If owns me, thinks he can take my place.'

A noise. We both sucked breath.

'Madness,' I whispered. 'Christ!'

'Christ,' Gerald snorted, 'has nothing . . . to do with it.' Vesalius blew a surprise of mirth.

'But *still*!'

'Shhh,' Gerald Vesalius cautioned.

'Was he like this when he first started to work for you?'

'I suppose. Not this bad.'

'It was okay then?'

'O'—a pause—'kay.'

'But—'

'As years passed he was more gree – gree – greedy.'

'For your cash?'

'No.' A derisive smile. 'My mind.'

'He'd steal *that*?'

Gerald sucked in, blew out. 'Imagine!'

'You're one of a kind!'

'Tell – tell – tell *him* that.'

'Son of a bitch!'

'No, jealous, envious, covetous, admiring, part monster, now monster full-time.' Gerald cried this in a few clear instants.

'Jesus,' I said. 'Why are we talking?'

'What else?' whispered Vesalius. 'Help.' He smiled.

'How will I get you out of here?'

Vesalius laughed. 'Let me count the ways.'

'No time for jokes, damn it!'

Gerald Vesalius swallowed. 'Have strange . . . sense' – he paused – 'humor. List!'

We both froze. A door creaked. Footsteps.

'Should I call the cops?'

'No.' A pause. Gerald's face writhed. 'Action, drama, wins!'

'Action?'

'Do as I say or all's lost.'

I bent close, he whispered frantically.

Whisper, whisper, whisper.

'Got that? Try?'

'Try!' I said. 'Oh, damn, damn, damn!'

Footsteps in the hall. I thought I heard someone yell. I grabbed the phone. I dialed.

I ran out the French doors, around the house, to the front walk.

A siren screamed, then a second and a third.

Three trucks of paramedic firemen booted up the walk with nothing else to do so late at night. Nine different paramedic firemen ran, eager not to be bored.

'Blair,' I yelled. 'That's me! Damn, I've locked myself out! Around the side! Man dying. Follow me.'

I ran. The black-suited paramedics blundered after.

We flung wide the French doors. I pointed at Vesalius.

'Out!' I cried. 'Brotman Hospital. Fast!'

They laid Gerald on a gurney and plunged out the French doors.

Behind us I heard Blair yelling hysterically.

Gerald Vesalius heard and waved gaily, calling out 'Ta-ta, toodle-o, farewell, solong, good-bye!' as we rushed toward the waiting ambulance.

Gerald whooped with laughter.

'Young man?'

'Gerald?'

'Do you love me?'

'Yes, Gerald.'

'But don't want to own me?'

'No, Gerald.'

'Not my mind?'

'No.'

'Not my body?'

'No, Gerald.'

'Till death do us part?'

'Till death do us part.'

'Good.'

Run, run, hustle, hustle, across the lawn, down the walk, toward the waiting ambulance.

'Young man.'

'Yes?'

'Vedanta Temple?'

'Yes.'

'Last year?'

'Yes.'

'Lecture on Great All Accepting Laughter?'

'I was there.'

'Well, *now's* the time!'

'Oh, yes, yes.'

'To hoot and holler?'

'Hoot and holler.'

'Zest and gusto, eh?'

'Gusto, zest, oh my God!'

Here a bomb burst in Gerald's chest and erupted from his throat. I'd never heard such jovial explosions in my life, and snort-laughed as I ran alongside Gerald as his gurney was hustled and hurried.

We howled, we shrieked, we yelled, we gasped, we insucked-outblew firecracker bomb-blasts of hilarity like boys on a forgotten summer day, collapsed on the sidewalk, writhing with comic seizures of wild upchuck heart attacks, throats choked, eyes clenched with brays of ha-hee and hee-ha and God, stop, I can't breathe, Gerald, hee-ha, ha-hee, and God, ha and hee, and once more ha-hee and whistle-rustle whisper haw.

'Young man?'

'What?'

'King Tut's mummy.'

'Yes?'

'Found in tomb.'

'Yes.'

'His mouth smiling.'

'Why?'

'In his front teeth—'

'Yes?'

'A single black hair.'

'What?'

'Dying man ate a hearty meal. Ha-ho!'

Hee-ha, oh my God, ha-hee, rush run, run rush.

'And now, one last thing.'

'What?'

'Will you run away with me?'

'Where?'

'Run off and be pirates!'

'What?'

'Run away with me to be pirates.'

We were at the ambulance, the doors were flung wide, Gerald was shoved in.

'Pirates!' he cried again.

'Oh God, yes, Gerald, I'll run off with you!'

Door slam, siren sound, motor gunned.

'Pirates!' I cried.

Pietà Summer

'Gosh, I can hardly wait!' I said.

'Why don't you shut up?' my brother replied.

'I can't sleep,' I said. 'I can't believe what's happening tomorrow. Two circuses in just one day! Ringling Brothers coming in on that big train at five in the morning, and Downey Brothers coming by truck a couple hours later. I can't stand it.'

'Tell you what,' my brother said. 'Go to sleep. We gotta get up at four-thirty.'

I rolled over but I just couldn't sleep because I could hear those circuses coming over the edge of the world, rising with the sun.

Before we knew it, it was 4:30 A.M. and my brother and I were up in the cold darkness, getting dressed, grabbing an apple for breakfast, and then running out in the street and heading down the hill toward the train yards.

As the sun began to rise the big Ringling Brothers and Barnum & Bailey train of ninety-nine cars loaded with elephants, zebras, horses, lions, tigers, and acrobats arrived; the huge engines steaming in the dawn, puffing out great clouds of black smoke, and the freight cars sliding open to let the horses hoof out into the darkness, and the elephants stepping down, very carefully, and the zebras, in huge striped flocks, gathering in the dawn, and my brother and I standing there, shivering, waiting for the parade to start, for there *was* going to be a parade of all the animals up through the dark morning town toward the distant acres where the tents would whisper upward toward the stars.

Sure enough my brother and I walked with the parade up the hill and through the town that didn't know we were there. But there we were, walking with ninety-nine elephants and one hundred zebras and two hundred horses, and the big bandwagon, soundless, out to the meadow that was nothing at all, but suddenly began to flower with the big tents sliding up.

Our excitement increased by the minute because where just hours ago there had been nothing at all, now there was everything in the world.

By seven-thirty Ringling Brothers and Barnum & Bailey had pretty well got its tents up and it was time for me and my brother to race back to where the motorcars were unloading the tiny Downey Brothers circus; a miniature version of the large miracle, it poured out of trucks instead of trains, with only ten elephants instead of nearly one hundred, and just a few zebras, and the lions, drowsing in their separate cages, looked old and mangy and exhausted. That applied to the tigers, too, and the camels that looked as if they'd been walking a hundred years, their pelts beginning to drop off.

My brother and I worked through the morning carrying cases of Coca-Cola, in real glass bottles, instead of plastic, so that lugging one of those cases meant carrying fifty pounds. By nine o'clock in the morning I was exhausted because I had had to move forty or more cases, taking care to avoid being trampled by one of the monster elephants.

At noon we raced home for a sandwich and then back to the small circus for two hours of explosions, acrobats, trapeze performers, mangy lions, clowns, and Wild West horse riding.

With the first circus done, we raced home and tried to rest, had another sandwich, then walked back to the big circus with our father at eight o'clock.

Another two hours of brass thunder followed, avalanches of sound and racing horses, expert marksmen, and a cage full of truly irritable and brand-new dangerous lions. At some point my brother ran off, laughing, with some friends, but I stayed fast by my father's side.

By ten o'clock the avalanches and explosions came to

a stunned halt. The parade I had witnessed at dawn was now reversed, and the tents were sighing down to lie like great pelts on the grass. We stood at the edge of the circus as it exhaled, collapsed its tents, and began to move away in the night, the darkness filled with a procession of elephants huffing their way back to the train yard. My father and I stood there, quiet, watching.

I put my right foot forward to start the long walk home when, suddenly, a strange thing happened: I went to sleep on my feet. I didn't collapse, I felt no terror, but quite suddenly I simply could not move. My eyes clamped shut and I began to fall, when suddenly I felt strong arms catch me and I was lifted into the air. I could smell the warm nicotine breath of my father as he cradled me in his arms, turned, and began the long shuffling walk home.

Incredible, the whole thing, for we were more than a mile from our house and it was truly late and the circus had almost vanished and all its strange people were gone.

On that empty sidewalk my father marched, cradling me in his arms for that great distance, impossible, for after all I was a thirteen-year-old boy weighing ninety-two pounds.

I could feel his difficult gasps as he gripped me, yet I could not fully wake. I struggled to blink my eyes and move my arms, but soon I was fast asleep and for the next half hour I had no way of knowing that I was being toted, a strange burden, through a town that was dousing its lights.

From far off I vaguely heard voices and someone saying, 'Come sit down, rest for a moment.'

I struggled to listen and felt my father jolt and sit. I sensed that somewhere on the homeward journey we had passed a friend's house and that the voice had called to my father to come rest on the porch.

We were there for five minutes, maybe more, my father holding me on his lap and me, still half asleep, listening to the gentle laughter of my father's friend, commenting on our strange odyssey.

At last the gentle laughter subsided. My father sighed, rose, and my half slumber continued. Half in and half out of dreams, I felt myself carried the final mile home.

The image I still have, seventy years later, is of my fine father, not for a moment making anything but a wry comment, carrying me through the night streets; probably the most beautiful memory a son ever had of someone who cared for him and loved him and didn't mind the long walk home through the night.

I've often referred to it, somewhat fancifully, as our pietà, the love of a father for his son – the walk on that long sidewalk, surrounded by those unlit houses as the last of the elephants vanished down the main avenue toward the train yards, where a locomotive whistled and the train steamed, getting ready to rush off into the night, carrying a tumult of sound and light that would live in my memory forever.

The next day I slept through breakfast, slept through the morning, slept through lunch, slept all afternoon, and finally wakened at five o'clock and staggered in to sit at dinner with my brother and my folks.

My father sat quietly, cutting his steak, and I sat across from him, examining my food.

'Papa,' I suddenly cried, tears falling from my eyes. 'Oh, thank you, Papa, thank you!'

My father cut another piece of steak and looked at me, his eyes shining very brightly.

'For what?' he said.

Fly Away Home

'Take good care. That's it, that's it.'

The cargo was most especially precious. It had been assembled and disassembled with the tenderest care here at the rocket port and given over to the workmen in immense packing cases, boxes as large as rooms, wrapped, double-wrapped, cottoned and serpentined and velveted over to prevent breakage. For all the tenderness and concern with the cartons and bales and parceled property, everyone rushed.

'On the double! Quick now!'

This was the Second Rocket. This was the Relief Rocket. The First Rocket had leaped up toward Mars the previous day. It was out booming now in the great black grasslands of space, lost from sight. And this Second Rocket must follow, as a bloodhound through a haunted moor, seeking a faint smell of iron and burned atom and phosphor. This Second Rocket, of a fat, overpacked size and shape, and with an odd and ridiculous series of people aboard, must not delay.

The Second Rocket was stuffed full. It trembled, shuddered, gathered itself like the hound of heaven, and bounded with a full and graceful leap, into the sky. It shook down avalanches of fire in its track. It rained coals and flame like furnaces suddenly heaven-borne. When the cinders died on the tarmac-concrete, the rocket was gone.

'Hope it gets there safely,' said a psychologist's aide, watching the sky.

The First Rocket arrived from a night sky and landed on the planet Mars. There was a great gasping sound as its machines drank of the cool air. After sniffing it through mechanical nostrils and lungs, the rocket pronounced the air of the finest vintage, ten million years old, intoxicating, but pure.

The rocket men stepped out.

They were alone.

Thirty men and a captain in a land where the wind blew forever across dust seas and around dead cities that had been dead when Earth was opening out like a jungle flower three times twenty million miles away. The sky was immensely clear, like a vat of crystal alcohol in which the stars blazed without a twinkle. The air knifed the throat and the lungs. You jerked it in with a gasp. It was thin, a ghost, gone when sought after. The men felt giddy and doubly alone. Sand moaned over their rocket. In time, said the night wind, if you stand quietly, I could bury you, as I did the stone cities and the mummified people hidden there, bury you like a needle and a few bright bits of thread, before you have a chance to make a pattern here.

'All right!' cried the captain, snapping it up.

The wind blew his voice away, end over end, a scrap of ghostly paper.

'Let's make a line there!' he cried against the loneliness.

The men moved in a numbed series of motions. They collided and milled and at last found their positions.

The captain faced them. The planet was under and all about them. They were at the bottom of a dry sea. A tide of years and centuries poured over and crushed them. They were the only living things here. Mars was dead and so far away from everything that a trembling began, imperceptibly, among them.

'Well,' cried the captain heartily. 'Here we are!'

'Here we are,' said a ghostly voice.

The men jerked about. Behind them, the walls of a half-buried town, a town dreamed full of dust and sand and old moss, a town that had drowned in time up to its highest turrets, tossed back an echo. The black walls quivered as running water does with sand.

'You all have your work to do!' cried the captain.

'To do,' said the city walls. 'To do.'

The captain showed his irritation. The men did not turn again, but the backs of their necks were cool and each hair felt separate and stirring.

'Sixty million miles,' whispered Anthony Smith, a corporal at the end of the line.

'No talking there!' cried the captain.

'Sixty million miles,' said Anthony Smith again, to himself, turning. In the cold dark sky, high above, Earth shone, a star, no more than a star, remote, beautiful, but only a star. There was nothing in the shape or the light to suggest a sea, a continent, a state, a city.

'Let's have it quiet!' shouted the captain angrily, surprised at his anger.

The men glanced down the line at Smith.

He was looking at the heavens. They looked where he looked and they saw Earth, infinitely removed over a distance of six months of time, and millions fired upon millions of miles in distance. Their thoughts whirled. Long years ago, men went to the arctic regions of Earth in boats, ships, balloons, and airplanes, took with them the bravest men, handpicked, psychologically clean, alert, the noncrackables, the well adjusted. But pick as they would, some men cracked, some went off into the arctic whiteness, into the long nights or the insanity of monthlong days. It was so alone. It was so alone. And herd-man, cut off from life, from women, from homes and towns, felt his mind melt away. Everything was bad and lonely.

'Sixty million miles!' said Anthony Smith, louder.

Then take thirty men. Shape, size, box, and parcel them. Antitoxin them, mind and body, purify and psycho-analyze, clap these hardies in a pistol, fire it at a target! At the end, in the final accounting, what do you have? You have thirty men in a line, one man beginning to talk under his breath, then louder, thirty men gazing up at the sky, seeing at a distant star, knowing that Illinois, Iowa, Ohio, and California are gone. Gone the cities, women, children, everything good, comfortable, and dear. Here you are, by God, on some terrible world where the wind never stops, where all is dead, where the captain is trying to be hearty. Suddenly, as if you had never considered it before, you say to yourself:

'Good Lord, I'm on Mars!'

Anthony Smith said it.

'I'm not home, I'm not on Earth, I'm on Mars! Where's Earth? There it is! See that damn small pinpoint of light? That's it! Isn't it silly? What're we doing here?'

The men stiffened. The captain jerked his head at Walton, the psychiatrist. They went down the line quickly, trying to be casual.

'All right, Smith, what seems to be the trouble?'

'I don't want to be here.' Smith's face was white. 'Good God, why did I come? This isn't Earth.'

'You took all the exams, you knew what you'd be up against.'

'No, I didn't. I blocked it off.'

The captain turned to the psychiatrist with a look of irritation and hatred, as if the doctor had failed. The doctor shrugged. 'Everyone makes mistakes,' he would have said, but stopped himself.

The young corporal was beginning to cry.

The psychiatrist turned instantly. 'Get to your jobs! Build a fire! Set up your tents! On the double!'

The men broke, mumbling. They walked off stiffly, looking back. 'Afraid of this,' said the psychiatrist. 'I was afraid. Space travel's so new, damn it. So *damn* new. No telling how many sixty million miles'll affect a person.' He took hold of the young corporal. 'Here we are. Everything's all right. You'd better get to your job, Corporal. Get busy. Get on the ball.'

The corporal had his hands to his face. 'It's a Christ-awful feeling. To know we're so far away from everything. And this whole damn planet is dead. Nothing else here but us.'

They started him unloading packets of frozen food.

The psychiatrist and the captain stood on a sand dune nearby for a moment, watching the men move.

'He's right, of course,' said the psychiatrist. 'I don't like it, either. It really hits you. It hits hard. It's lonely here. It's awfully dead and far away. And that wind. And the empty cities. I feel lousy.'

'I don't feel so well myself,' said the captain. 'What do you think? About Smith? Will he stay on this side of the cliff or will he fall over?'

'I'll stick with him. He needs friends now. If he falls over, I'm afraid he'll take some others with him. We're all tied together by ropes, even if you can't see them. I hope to hell the second rocket comes through. See you later.'

The psychiatrist went away and the rocket stood on the sea bottom in the night in the center of the planet Mars, as the two white moons rose suddenly, like terrors and memories, and flung themselves in a race over the sky. The captain stood looking up at the sky and Earth burning there.

During the night, Smith went mad. He fell over into darkness, but took no one with him. He pulled hard at the ropes, caused terrible secret panics all night, with screams, shouts, warning of terror and death. But the others stood firm positioned in the dark, working, perspiring. None was blown with him to his secret place at the bottom of a long cliff. He fell all night. He hit in the morning. Under sedatives, eyes shut, coiled upon himself, he was bunked in the ship, where his cries whispered away. There was silence, with only the wind and the men working. The psychiatrist passed extra rations of food, chocolate, cigarettes, brandy. He watched. The captain watched with him.

'I don't know. I'm beginning to think—'

'What?'

'Men were never meant to go so far alone. Space travel

asks too much. Isolation, completely unnatural, a form of realistic insanity, space itself, if you ask me,' said the captain. 'Watch out, I'm going balmy myself.'

'Keep talking,' said the doctor.

'What do you think? Can we stick it out here?'

'We'll hold on. The men look bad, I admit. If they don't improve in twenty-four hours, and if our relief ship doesn't show up, we'd best get back into space. Just knowing they're heading home will snap them out of it.'

'God, what a waste. What a shame. A billion dollars spent to send us. What do we tell the senators at home, that we were cowards?'

'At times, cowardice is the only thing left. A man can take only so much, then it's time for him to run, unless he can find someone to do his running for him. We'll see.'

The sun rose. The double moons were gone. But Mars was no more comfortable by day than by night. One of the men fired off a gun at some animal he saw behind him. Another stopped work with a blinding headache, and retired to the ship. Though they slept most of the day, it was a fitful sleeping, with many calls on the doctor for sedatives and brandy rations. At nightfall, the doctor and the captain conferred.

'We'd better pull out,' said Walton. 'This man Sorenson is another. I give him twenty-four hours. Ditto Bernard.

A damn shame. Good men, both of them. Fine men. But there was no way to duplicate Mars in our Earth offices. No test can duplicate the unknown. Isolation-shock, loneliness-shock, *severe*. Well, it was a good try. Better to be happy cowards than raving lunatics. Myself? I hate it here. As the man said, I want to go home.'

'Shall I give the order, then?' asked the captain.

The psychiatrist nodded.

'Jesus, God, I hate to give up without a fight.'

'Nothing to fight but wind and dust. We could give it a decent fight with the relief ship, but that doesn't seem to be—'

'Captain, sir!' someone shouted.

'Eh?' The captain and psychiatrist turned.

'Look there, sir! In the sky! The relief rocket!'

This was no more than the truth. The men ran out of the ship and the tents. The sun was set and the wind was cold, but they stood there, straining their eyes up, watched the fire grow large, larger, larger. The Second Rocket beat a drum and let out a long plume of red color. It landed. It cooled. The men of the First Rocket ran across the sea bottom toward it, yelling.

'Well?' asked the captain, standing back. 'What does this mean? Do we go or stay?'

'I think,' said the psychiatrist, 'that we'll stay.'

'For twenty-four hours?'

'For a little longer than that,' Walton replied.

* * *

They hoisted immense crates out of the Second Rocket.

'Careful! Careful there!'

They held up blueprints and wielded hammers and pries and levers. The psychiatrist supervised. 'This way! Crate 75? Here. Box 067? *Here!* That's it. Open 'er up. Tab A into Slot B. Tab B into Slot C. Right, fine, *good*!'

They put it all up before dawn. In eight hours they assembled the miracles out of boxes and crates. They took away the serpentines, wax papers, cardboards, brushed and dusted every part and portion of the whole. When the time came, the men of the First Rocket stood on the outer rim of the miracle, gazed in at it, incredulous and awed.

'Ready, Captain?'

'I'll be damned! Yes!'

'Throw the switch.'

The captain threw the switch.

The little town lit up.

'Good Lord!' said the captain.

He walked into the single main street of the town.

It was a street of no more than six buildings on a side, false fronts, strung with bright red, yellow, green lights. Music played from a half-dozen hidden jukeboxes, somewhere. Doors slammed. A man in a white smock emerged from a barbershop, blue shears and a black comb in hand. A peppermint-stick pole rotated slowly behind him. Next was a drugstore, a magazine rack out front, newspapers fluttering in the wind, a fan turning in the ceiling, the snakelike hiss of soda water sounding inside. As they passed the door they looked in. A girl smiled there, a crisp green starched cap on her head.

A pool hall, with green tables, like jungle glades, soft, inviting. Billiard balls, multicolored, triangled, waiting. Across the street, a church, with candied-root-beer, strawberry, lemon-glass windows. A man there, too, in dark suit, white collar. Next to that, a library. Next to that, a hotel. SOFT BEDS. FIRST NIGHT FREE. AIR-CONDITIONING. A clerk behind a desk with his hand on a silver bell. But the place they were going to, that drew them like the smell of water draws cattle across a dusty prairie, was the building at the head of the street.

THE MILLED BUCK SALOON.

A man with greased, curled hair, his shirtsleeves gartered with red elastic above his hairy elbows, leaned against a post there. He vanished behind swinging doors. When they hit the swinging doors, he was polishing the bar and tipping rye into thirty glasses all lined up glittering on the beautiful long bar. A crystal chandelier blazed warmly overhead. There was a stairway leading up and a number of doors above, on a balcony, and the faintest smell of perfume.

They all went to the bar. They were quiet. They took up the rye and drank it straight down, not wiping their mouths. Their eyes stung.

The captain said, in a whisper, to the psychiatrist, standing by the door, 'Good God! The expense!'

'Film sets, knockdowns, collapsibles. A real minister next door in the church of course. Three real barbers. A piano player.'

The man at the yellow-toothed piano began to play 'St. Louis Woman with Your Diamond Rings.'

'A druggist, two fountain girls, a pool-hall proprietor, shoeshine boy, rack boy, two librarians, odds and ends, workmen, electricians, et cetera. Totals up another two million dollars. The hotel is *all* real. Every room with bath. Comfort. Good beds. Other buildings are three-quarters false front. All of it so beautifully constructed, with slots and tabs, a child could put up the whole toy-works in an hour.'

'But will it work?'

'Look at their faces, beginning to relax already.'

'Why didn't you tell me?!'

'Because, if it'd got out, spending money this silly, ridiculous way, the papers would've jumped me – senators, Congress, God would have gotten in the act. It's silly, damn silly, but it *works*. It's *Earth*. That's all I care about. It's *Earth*. It's a piece of Earth the men can hold in their hand and say, "This is Illinois, this is a town I *knew*. These are *buildings* I knew. This is a little piece of Earth that's here for me to hold on to until we bring *more* of it up and make the loneliness run away forever."'

'Ingenious, devilish, clever.'

The men ordered a second rye all around, smiling.

'The men on our ship, Captain, are from fourteen

small towns. Picked them that way. One of each of these buildings in this little street here is from one of those towns. The bartender, ministers, grocery-store owner, all thirty of the people on the Second Rocket, are from those towns.'

'Thirty? *Besides* the relief crew?'

The psychiatrist glanced happily at the steps leading up to the balcony and the series of shut doors. One of the doors opened a trifle and a beautiful blue eye gazed out for a moment.

'We'll rush in more lights and more towns every month, more people, more Earth. Priority on familiarity. Familiarity breeds sanity. We've won the first round. We'll keep winning if we keep moving.'

Now the men were beginning to laugh and talk and slap one another on the shoulders. Some of them walked out and across the street for a haircut, some went to play pool, some to buy groceries, some into the quiet church, you could hear organ music for a moment just before the piano player here in the crystal-chandeliered saloon began 'Frankie and Johnny.' Two men walked laughingly up the stairs to the doors along the balcony.

'I'm no drinking man, Captain. How about a pineapple malt at the drugstore over the way?'

'What? Oh. I was thinking . . . Smith.' The captain turned. 'Back in the ship. Do you think – I mean – could we get Smith, bring him here, with us, would it do any good, would he *like* it, mightn't it make him *happy*?'

'We could certainly try,' said the doctor.

The pianist was playing, very loud, 'That Old Gang of Mine.' Everybody singing, some of them starting to dance, and the city like a jewel blazing in the wilderness, darkness all around. Mars lonely, the sky black and full of stars, the wind rushing, the moons rising, the seas and old cities dead. But the barber pole whirled brightly, and the church windows were the color of Coca-Cola and lemonade and boysenberry phosphate.

The piano was tinkling 'Skip to My Lou' half an hour later when the captain, the psychiatrist, and a third man walked into the drugstore and sat.

'Three pineapple malts,' said the captain.

And they sat, reading magazines, turning slowly on the stools, until the girl behind the fountain set three beautiful pineapple malts at their elbows.

They all reached for the straws.

Un-pillow Talk

'Good Lord.'

'Good Lord, indeed!'

They fell back and stared at the ceiling. There was a long pause in which they regained their breath.

'That was wonderful,' she said.

'Wonderful,' he said.

There was another pause while they examined the ceiling.

Finally she said, 'Wonderful, but—'

'What do you mean "but"?' he said.

'It was wonderful,' she said. 'But now we've ruined everything.'

'Ruined?'

'Our friendship,' she said. 'It was such a great thing and now we've lost it.'

'I don't believe that,' he said.

She examined the ceiling in even more detail.

'Yes,' she said, 'it was so marvelous. It went on for a long time. What was it, a year? And now, like damn fools, we've killed it.'

'We weren't damn fools,' he said.

'That's how I see it. In a moment of weakness.'

'No, passion,' he said.

'No matter how you put it,' she said, 'we've spoiled everything. How long ago was it? A year? We were great pals, fine buddies, went to the library together, played tennis, drank beer instead of champagne, and now we let one little hour throw it all overboard.'

'I don't buy that,' he said.

'Think about it,' she said. 'Stop and examine the last hour and the last year. You've gotta come around to my way of thinking.'

He watched the ceiling to see if he could see there any of the things she had just said.

At last he sighed.

She heard the sigh and said, 'Does that mean yes, you agree?'

He nodded and she felt the nod.

They both lay on their separate pillows, staring at the ceiling for a long while.

'How do we get it back?' she said. 'It's so stupid. We've known better than this with other people. We've seen how things can be killed and yet we went right ahead and killed it. Do you have any ideas? What do we do now?'

'Get out of bed,' he said, 'and have an early breakfast.'

'That won't do it,' she said. 'Hold still for a while, maybe something will come to us.'

'But I'm hungry,' he said.

'I'm more than hungry, I'm ravenous. For answers, that is.'

'What are you doing? What's that sound?'

'I think I'm crying. What a terrible loss. Yes, I think I'm crying.'

They lay for another long moment and then he stirred.

'I've got a crazy idea,' he said.

'What?'

'If we lie here with our heads on our pillows and look at the ceiling and talk about the last hour and then the last week to see how we led up to this, and then the last month and the whole last year, mightn't that help?'

'In what way?' she said.

'We'll *un*-pillow talk,' he said.

'Un what?'

'Un-pillow talk. We've heard of pillow talk all our lives, the talk that goes on late at night or early morning. Pillow talk between husbands and wives and lovers. But in this case maybe we can put everything in reverse. If we can talk our way back to where we were last night at ten o'clock, and then at six, and then at noon, maybe somehow we can talk the whole thing away. Un-pillow talk.'

She made the smallest sound of laughter.

'I guess we could try,' she said. 'What do we do?'

'Well, we'll just lie very straight and relax and look at the ceiling with our heads on our pillows and we'll start to talk.'

'What's the first thing we talk about?'

'Shut your eyes and just say anything you want to say.'

'But *not* about tonight,' she said. 'If we talk about the last hour, we might get into even worse trouble.'

'Forget the last hour,' he said, 'or remember it quickly, and then let's get back to *early* in the evening.'

She lay very straight and shut her eyes and held her fists at her sides.

'I think it was the candles,' she said.

'The candles?'

'I shouldn't have bought them. I shouldn't have lit them. It was our first candlelit dinner. Not only that, but champagne instead of beer; that was a big mistake.'

'Candles,' he said. 'Champagne. Yeah.'

'It was late. Usually you go home early. We break it up and get together early mornings to play tennis or to head to the library. But you stayed awfully late and we opened that second bottle of champagne.'

'No more second bottles,' he said.

'I'll throw out the candles,' she said. 'But before that, what kind of year has it been?'

'Really great,' he said. 'I've never known a greater pal, a greater buddy, a greater companion.'

'Same goes here,' she said. 'Where did we meet?'

'You know. It was the library. I saw you prowling the stacks almost every day I was there, for about a week. You seemed to be looking for something. Maybe it wasn't a book.'

'Well then,' she said. 'Maybe it was *you* after all. I saw you wandering the stacks, saw you studying the books. The first thing you said to me was, "How about Jane Austen?" What a peculiar thing for a man to say. Most men don't read Jane Austen, or if they did they wouldn't admit it or open a conversation with a line like that.'

'That wasn't a line,' he said. 'I thought you looked like a reader of Jane Austen, or maybe even Edith Wharton. It was quite natural.'

'From there,' she said, 'it really opened out. I remember we began to walk through the stacks together and you pulled out a special edition of Edgar Allan Poe to show me, and though I never was a Poe fan, the way you talked about him, the way you inspired me, I began to read the awful man the next day.'

'So,' he said, 'it was Austen and Wharton and Poe. Those are great names for a literary company.'

'And then you asked me if I played tennis and I said yes. You said you were better at badminton but you'd try tennis with me. So we played against each other and that was great . . . I think one of the mistakes we made was that this week, for the first time ever, we played doubles and we played together against the other two.'

'Yes, that was a great mistake. As long as I opposed you, there was no chance for any candles or any champagne. Maybe that's not strictly true, but you beating me all the time, I must admit, made it difficult.'

She laughed quietly. 'Well then, I have to admit that when we became a team on the court and won the game yesterday, not long after that, without thinking, I went out and bought the candles.'

'Good God,' he said.

'Yes,' she said. 'Isn't life strange?' She paused and looked at the ceiling again. 'Are we almost there?'

'Where?'

'Back where we should be. Back a year ago, a month ago, hell, even a week ago. I'd settle even for that.'

'Keep talking,' he said.

'No, you,' she said. 'You've got to help.'

'Well then, it was those days driving up the coast and back. We never stayed overnight. We just loved the drive in the open car with the wind and the sea and there was one hell of a lot of laughter.'

'Yes,' she said. 'That's it, isn't it? When you think back about all your friends and all the most important times in your life, laughter is the greatest gift. We did much of that.'

'You actually went to some of my lectures and didn't fall asleep.'

'How could I? You've always been brilliant.'

'No,' he said. 'A genius, yes, but not brilliant.'

She laughed again, quietly.

'You've been reading too much Bernard Shaw lately.'

'Does it show?'

'Yes, but I don't mind. Genius or brilliant, the talk has been fine.'

'How are we doing?' he said.

'I think we're getting close,' she said. 'I'm almost back to six months ago. If we keep going, it will be a year. And tonight will be just some sort of bright, wonderful, dumb memory.'

'Well put,' he said. 'Keep talking.'

'Another thing,' she said. 'In all our travels, from breakfast at the seaside to lunch in the mountains to dinner in Palm Springs, we were always home before midnight – me dropped off at the door and you driving off.'

'That's right. What wonderful trips. Well now,' he said, 'how do you feel?'

'I think I'm there,' she said. 'This un-pillow talk was a great idea.'

'Are you back in the library and walking, all by yourself?'

'Yes.'

'I'll follow after a while,' he said. 'Just one more thing.'

'Yes?'

'At noon tomorrow, tennis, but this time you're across the net again and we play against each other, like in the old days, and I'll win and you'll lose.'

'Don't be so sure. Noon. Tennis. Just like the old times. Anything else?'

'Don't forget to buy the beer.'

'Beer,' she said. 'Yes. Now what? Friends?'

'What?'

'Friends?'

'Of course.'

'Good. Now, I'm very tired; I need sleep, but I'm feeling better.'

'Me, too,' he said.

'So, my head's on the pillow, your head's on yours, but before we go to sleep there's one more thing.'

'What?'

'Can I hold your hand? Just that.'

'Of course.'

'Because I have a terrible feeling,' she said, 'that the bed might spin and you'll be thrown off and I'll wake up to find you're not holding my hand.'

'Hold on,' he said.

His hand touched hers. They lay very straight, very still.

'Good night,' he said.

'Oh, yes, good, good night,' she said.

Come Away with Me

Why Joseph Kirk did what he did, on impulse, he could not immediately say. He could only recall, instantaneously, similar incidents that had caused him to erupt years ago.

At a small private dinner, when an obnoxious film producer had bragged about 'selling out,' implying that *everyone* did, Joseph Kirk had put down his knife and fork and ordered the producer away from the table. The producer obeyed.

On another occasion, when a film actress verbally whiplashed her husband for half an hour in front of guests, Kirk had jumped up, told her how awful she was, and walked off to the next room to read a book. On the way out, later, she apologized and he looked the other way.

Now, tonight, it had happened again. He heard himself saying an incredible thing. It was as if someone had handed him a grenade and, thoughtless, he had yanked the ring and gripped the damned thing, staring, as it went off.

He was browsing at a newsstand in the early evening, leafing through a few magazines, when he heard angry voices approaching. One high, shrill, and derogatory; the other smothered, half mute, already defeated. The newsstand was south of Hollywood Boulevard, and the voices came from that direction.

Joseph Kirk glanced from the corners of his eyes. What he saw was one handsome young man striding along, hurling insults as if they were favors over his shrugged shoulder. He seemed to be wearing an invisible cape. He seemed to be wearing a mask. But that wasn't true, either; it was just the way he held his face, in a frozen grimace of hauteur as he manufactured his diatribes.

Behind him, smaller, meeker, and most certainly not louder, came his friend with an equally handsome face, but no invisible cape, no mask, just a face like someone out in the rain and bewildered by the storm.

'My God,' cried the first young man, glaring at the street ahead, 'you never do *anything* right!'

'What did I do now?'

'Last night, this morning, just now. You behave like a cow. Can't you be polite? Can't you act properly? At that party, my God! Can't you smile, or laugh, or make small talk? Stood around like a damned wooden Indian!'

'I—'

'And today at lunch, with Teddy trying to amuse us, hilarious, and you just sat there. Jesus! You—'

The parade of two went by, the first part pompous, tall, and glorious in its feline display, the second part defeated, dragging, and lost. The hackles on the back of Kirk's neck rose and rippled down his back. He found himself grinding his teeth and shutting his eyes.

'Then this afternoon. Do you know what you *did* this afternoon?'

'What did I do, what did I *do*?'

'You—'

'Oh, shut up!' cried Kirk.

The world froze. The parade stopped. Its pompous half whirled as if shot through the heart. His defeated friend stood motionless, slowly lifting his head with a look of dismay mixed with curious relief.

'What?' cried the man with the invisible mask.

Kirk felt his mouth move and, still disbelieving his own outburst, continued. 'I said shut up.'

'And who the hell are you?' cried the first young man.

'Nobody at all, but damn it all to hell!'

Where am I going with this? Kirk wondered. And then he looked at the second young man's face and saw an answer. There was a burgeoning of hope there, a wonder, and a need to escape.

'Look,' said Kirk. 'You're coming with *me*.'

'What?' said the second young man.

'You don't really want to be with this monster, do you?' said Kirk. 'No. No, come along. I'll make you happier than he can. I'll start by leaving you alone. We'll go on from there, yes? Well? Him or me?'

The second young man stood riven, blinking from his friend to Kirk, and then at the ground, unable to choose.

'Look here,' said the first young man, his mask beginning to melt. 'You—'

'No.' Kirk put his hand out to touch the second young man's elbow. 'Freedom at last. Isn't it glorious? Get out of the way, *you*! Come along, *you*.'

He stepped between them quickly, and spun the second man about and walked him off.

'You can't *do* that!' cried the other, stunned.

'Watch my dust!' shouted Kirk.

And he kept walking with his captive to and around the corner, swiftly, with the cries of the cormorant or the shrike or whatever it was, echoing behind.

'Keep walking,' said Kirk.

'I am.'

'Don't look back.'

'I'm not.'

'Faster.'

'I'm running.'

'Good.'

They made it to the next corner and stopped for a moment, staring at each other.

'Who are you?' the second young man asked.

'Your savior, I guess.'

'Why did you do that?'

'I don't know. I had to. It was awful.'

'What's your name?'

'Kirk. Joseph Kirk.'

'I'm Willy-Bob.'

'Jesus Christ. You *look* like a Willy-Bob.'

'I know. Will he come after us?'

'He's probably in shock right now. Let's keep moving. My car's down here.'

They made it to the car, and while Kirk was unlocking the passenger-side door, Willy-Bob said: 'Lord, you're not even one of us! You're not even . . . *you* know.'

There was a long silence while they got into the car. Before Kirk started the engine, he heard Willy-Bob say, '*Are* you?'

Kirk turned to look at him, laughing quietly. 'No.'

'Then, why, *why*?'

'Letting you go on down the street with that son of a bitch drove me wild. I couldn't let it happen.'

'I love him, you know.'

'Yeah, and more's the pity. But, you're with *me* now.'

'What are you going to do with me?'

'I'm a man without a nose. You're a box of Kleenex. I'll think of something.'

Kirk began to laugh. Willy-Bob joined him.

'Oh, this is incredible. This is rich!'

Tears ran down both their faces.

'Isn't it?' said Kirk, and drove away with his captive.

They found a drive-in and finished their laughing there. They ordered two hamburgers, french fries, and two beers and sat waiting to let the laughter die.

'My God, his face! Christ, I feel good,' cried Willy-Bob.

'That's what I intended,' said Kirk.

'It's the first time, the first time I ever spoke up in my life!'

But you didn't, thought Kirk, but let it go.

'I can just imagine him, right now, stomping up and down the boulevard, trying to find me, furious . . .'

Willy-Bob's voice began to fade. 'Jesus, when he *does* find me! All my stuff is back at his place.'

'It's not *your* place, too?'

'We share an apartment over on Fountain.'

'How much junk you got there?'

'A lot. Change of clothes. A toilet kit. Beat-up old typewriter. I guess there's nothing there.'

'Not much,' said Kirk.

The hamburgers arrived in time to interrupt a growing silence. They ate quietly. Half through his sandwich, Willy-Bob swallowed hard and said, 'Well, again, what are you going to do with me?'

'Nothing.'

'You can, you know. I owe you.'

'You don't owe me anything. You owe yourself some-thing. To get the hell out, to get the hell away.'

'You're right. Still, I don't understand, why did you do it, why am I here with you?'

Kirk took another bite and ruminated, his eyes on the windshield, where bugs had struck and died. He tried to read their dried juices.

'Two dogs get joined, middle of the street, can't get free, I run out, hose them down. Barn owl in a field, fallen from a tree, took it home, gave it warm milk. Hell.'

'Am I a barn owl out of a tree?'

'There's a remarkable resemblance.'

'I still can't fly.'

'That's why I spoke up.'

'But you didn't know anything *about* me.'

'Yes, I did, seeing you go by. *Listening* to you.'

'You didn't know anything about *him*.'

'I did, seeing *him* walk by, hearing his whole life, and yours.'

'You're awfully good at seeing and hearing.'

'It's no virtue. Makes trouble. Look at us here, me and you. What next?'

They finished their sandwiches and worked on their beers, and Willy-Bob said, 'Maybe we could have a life together . . .'

'No way,' said Kirk abruptly, and stopped. 'I mean, I'm just a down-at-the-heels analyst, a damn-fool ham-fisted do-gooder, in this up to my chin and as uncomfortable as you are. We have no true use for one another. The only thing holding us together is my pity and your fear.'

'That'll have to do,' said Willy-Bob. 'Do I go home with you tonight? That is, *if* I go home with you.'

'You're sounding more doubtful every second.'

'I'm scared as hell. Feel as if I had thrown up in church.'

'God will *never* forgive you, will He?'

'He never has.'

Kirk drank his beer. 'Your guy isn't God, he's Lucifer. And his apartment is hell on Earth. You might as well blow your brains out as go back.'

'I know.' Willy-Bob nodded, eyes shut.

'Yet you're thinking about it, right now?'

'I am.'

'Let's find you a room for the night. Being somewhere different may give you more—'

'Courage?'

'Hell, I don't want to preach.'

'God, I *need* preaching. A hotel, yes. But I've no money—'

'I think I can afford it,' said Kirk.

Kirk started the car and Willy-Bob said, 'On the way, if it isn't far, could we drive by your place, so I could see—'

'What?'

'From outside, the house you live in, you *are* married, aren't you? It would be nice to see some place permanent. I mean, just drive by, okay?'

'Well,' said Kirk.

'Okay?' said Willy-Bob.

They drove, circling, through Hollywood. Along the way, Kirk said, 'You have a job? No. I'll bring you the want ads tomorrow, so you can live alone awhile and find out who the hell you really are. How long you been living, if you can call it that, with that son of a bitch?'

'A year. The greatest year in my life. A year. The most horrible year in my life.'

'Half and half. I know the feeling.'

They arrived at and moved slowly past the front of Kirk's small white bungalow. An apricot-colored lamp shone in the front window. It looked warm, even to Kirk, as they almost stopped.

'Is that it, your window?' asked Willy-Bob. 'It looks great.'

'It's all right.'

'God, you're a nice man. What's wrong with me I can't relax and be saved? What's wrong?!' Willy-Bob wailed, and burst into tears.

Kirk handed over a Kleenex and then impulsively leaned across and kissed Willy-Bob on the forehead. Willy-Bob's face, tear-streaked, came up swiftly, surprised.

Kirk pulled back. 'No offense. No offense!'

They both laughed and circled back through Hollywood to find a small hotel.

Kirk got out of the car.

'You better get back in,' said Willy-Bob.

'You're not staying here now?'

'You know I can't.'

Kirk stood waiting. At last Willy-Bob said: 'Did you have a lot of girlfriends?'

'A few.'

'I should think so. You're nice-looking. And you behave nicely. Is your marriage happy? Does niceness help that?'

'I'm all right,' said Kirk. 'I miss the way it once was, when we started out.'

'Oh, I wish I could miss *him* sometime and get it over with. I'm sick to my stomach now.'

'It'll pass, if you give it a chance.'

'No.' Willy-Bob shook his head. 'It will never pass.'

That did it.

Kirk climbed back in and sat for a moment watching the young, fragile man dry his tears.

'Where do you want me to take you?'

'I'll show you the place.'

Kirk put the keys in the ignition and waited. 'The hotel is here. Last chance for life. Going, going, gone. Nine-eight-seven . . .'

Kirk looked at the beer Willy-Bob was holding. Willy-Bob laughed quietly.

'The condemned man drank a hearty meal.'

He crumpled the can, threw it out. 'Now it's just junk, like me. Well?'

Kirk swallowed a curse and started the car.

'There he is!'

They had driven along Santa Monica Boulevard and approached a place called the Blue Parrot. Out front, half in, half out the door, stood the man with the invisible mask and the unseen cape. Right now his mask hung half off his face, his eyes damaged, his mouth wounded, but there he stood, anyway, arms crossed over his chest, foot tapping impatiently.

When he saw Kirk's car slow and saw who was in the passenger seat, his whole body toppled forward eagerly. But then his mask sank back in place, his spine straightened, his arms crushed his chest firmly as his chin came up and his eyes blazed in silence.

Kirk stopped the car. 'You sure you want to be here?'

'Yes,' said Willy-Bob, eyes down, hands tucked between his legs.

'You know what's going to happen, don't you? It'll be hell for the next week, or, if I read him right, the next month.'

'I know.' Willy-Bob's head nodded quietly.

'And yet you want to go to him?'

'It's the only thing I can do.'

'No, you can stay at the hotel and I'll buy you a compass.'

'What kind of future is that?' said Willy-Bob. 'You don't love me.'

'No, I don't. Now, jump out and run like hell, *alone*!'

'Christ, don't you think I'd *like* to do that?'

'Do it, then. For me. For you. Run. Find someone else.'

'There *is* no one else, in the whole world. He loves me, you know. If I left him, it'd kill him.'

'And if you go back, he'll kill *you*.' Kirk took a deep breath and let it out in a sigh. 'God, I feel like someone's drowning and I'm throwing him an anvil.'

Willy-Bob's fingers toyed with the door handle. The door sprang open. The man standing in the Blue Parrot doorway saw this. Again, the toppled move of his body, again the return of balance, as a grim line formed around his death-rictus mouth.

Willy-Bob slid out of the car, the bones in his body dissolving as he went. By the time he stood full on the pavement, he seemed a foot shorter than he had been ten minutes ago. He leaned down and peered anxiously in through the car window as if talking to a judge in a traffic court.

'You don't understand.'

'I do,' said Kirk. 'And that's the sad part.'

He reached out and patted Willy-Bob's cheek. 'Try to have a good life, Willy-Bob.'

'*You've* already had one. I'll always remember you,' said Willy-Bob. 'Thanks for trying.'

'Used to be a lifeguard. Maybe I'll head down to the beach tonight, climb up on the station, be on the lookout for more drowning bodies.'

'Do that,' said Willy-Bob. 'Save someone worth saving. Good night.'

Willy-Bob turned and headed for the Blue Parrot.

His friend, the man with the now-restored mask and flamboyant cape, had gone inside, secure, certain, without waiting. Willy-Bob blinked at the flapping hinged doors until they stood still. Then, head down in the rain that no one else saw, he walked across the sidewalk.

Kirk didn't wait. He gunned the motor and drove away.

He reached the ocean in twenty minutes, stared at the empty lifeguard station in the moonlight, listened to the surf, and thought, Hell, there's no one out there to be saved, and drove home.

He climbed into bed with the last of the beer and drank it slowly, staring at the ceiling until his wife, head turned toward the wall, at last said, 'Well, what have you been up to, *this* time?'

He finished the beer, lay back, and shut his eyes.

'Even if I told you,' he said, 'you wouldn't believe it.'

Apple-core Baltimore

On the way to the cemetery Menville decided they
needed to pick up something to eat, so they stopped the
car at a roadside stand near an orange grove where there
were displays of bananas, apples, blueberries, and, of
course, oranges.

Menville picked out two wonderful, big, glossy apples
and handed one to Smith.

Smith said, 'How come?'

Menville, looking enigmatic, just said, 'Eat, eat.' They
stowed their jackets in the car and walked the rest of
the way to the graveyard.

Once inside the gates, they walked a great distance
until at last they came to a special marker.

Smith looked down and said, 'Russ Simpson. Wasn't
he an old friend of yours from high school?'

'Yeah,' said Menville. 'That was the one. Part of the gang. My very best friend, actually. Russ Simpson.'

They stood for a while, biting into their apples, chewing quietly.

'He must have been very special,' Smith said. 'You've come all this way. But you didn't bring any flowers.'

'No, only these apples. You'll see.'

Smith stared at the marker. 'What was there about him that was so special?'

Menville took another bite of his apple and said, 'He was *constant*. He was there every noon, he was there on the streetcar going to school and then back home every day. He was there at recess, he sat across from me in homeroom, and we took a class in the short story together. It was that kind of thing. Oh, sure, on occasion he did crazy stuff.'

'Like what?' said Smith.

'Well, we had this little gang of five or six guys who met at lunchtime. We were all different, but on the other hand, we were all sort of the same. Russ used to sort of pick at me, you know how friends do.'

'Pick? Like what?'

'He liked to play a game. He'd look at all of us and say, "Someone say 'Granger.'" He'd look at me and say, "Say 'Granger.'" I'd say "Granger" and Russ would shake his head and say, "No, no. One of you others say 'Granger.'" So one of the other guys would say "Granger" and they would all laugh, a big reaction, because he said "Granger" just the right way. Then Russ would turn to me and say, "Now it's your turn, you say it." I would say "Granger" and no one would laugh and I'd stand there, feeling left out.

'There was a trick to the whole thing but I was so stupid, so naive, that I could never figure out that it was a joke, the sort of thing they played on me.

'Then one time I was over at Russ's house and a friend of his named Pipkin leaned over the balcony in the living room and dropped a cat on me. Can you believe that?! The cat landed right on my head and clawed my face. It could have put out my eyes, I thought later. Russ thought it was a great joke. Russ was laughing and Pip was laughing, and I threw the cat across the room. Russ was indignant. "Watch what you're doing with the cat!" he said. "Watch what the cat was doing with me!" I cried. That was a big joke; he told everyone. They all laughed, except me.'

'That's some memory,' said Smith.

'He was there every day, was in school with me, my best friend. Every once in a while, at lunchtime, he'd eat an apple and when he finished he'd say, "Apple core." And one of the other guys would say, "Baltimore." Russ would then say, "Who's your friend?" They'd point at me and he'd throw the apple core – hard – at me. This was a routine; it happened at least once a week for a couple of years. Apple-core Baltimore.'

'And this was your best friend?'

'Sure, my best friend.'

They stood there by the grave, still working at their apples. The sun was getting hotter and there was no breeze.

'What else?' said Smith.

'Oh, not much. Well, sometimes at lunchtime I'd ask the typing teacher to let me use one of the typewriters so I could write, as I didn't have a typewriter of my own.

'Finally, I had a chance to buy one real cheap, so I went without lunch for a month or so, saving my lunch money. Finally, I had enough to buy my very own typewriter so I could write whenever I wanted.

'One day Russ looked at me and said, "My God, do you realize what you are?" I said, "What?" He said, "You're a stale fruitcake, giving up your money to buy that damned typewriter. A stale fruitcake."

'I often thought later that someday when I finished my great American novel, that's what I'd call it: *Stale Fruitcake*.'

Smith said, 'Better than *Gatsby*, huh?'

'*Gatsby*, sure. Anyway, I had the typewriter.'

They were quiet then, the only sound the last bites into their diminishing apples.

A distant expression came over Smith's face and he blinked and suddenly whispered, 'Apple-core.'

To which, quickly, Menville said, 'Baltimore.'

Smith then said, 'Who's your friend?'

Menville, looking down at the marker near his feet, eyes wide, said, 'Granger.'

'Granger?' said Smith, and stared at his friend.

'Yeah,' said Menville. 'Granger.'

At this Smith raised his hand and threw his apple core down on top of the gravestone.

No sooner was this done than Menville hurled his apple core down, then reached and took it up again and threw it a second time so that the gravestone was so littered with shreds of the apple core that you couldn't make out the name on the marker.

They stared at the mess.

Then Menville turned and began to walk away, threading through the gravestones, tears streaming down his cheeks.

Smith called after him. 'Where are you going?'

Menville, not looking back, said in a hoarse voice, 'To get some more apples, damn it to hell, more apples.'

The Reincarnate

After a while you will get over being afraid. There's nothing you can do; just be careful to walk at night.

The sun is terrible; summer nights are no help. You must wait for cold weather. The first six months are your prime. In the seventh month the water will seep through with dissolution. By the eighth month your usefulness will fade. Come the tenth month you'll lie weeping in sorrow without tears, and you will know then that you will never move again.

But before that happens there is so much to be finished. Many likes and dislikes must be turned in your mind before your mind melts.

It is all new to you. You are reborn! And your birthplace is silk lined and smells of tuberoses and linens, and there is no sound before your birth except the beating of the earth's billion insect hearts. This place is wood and metal and satin, offering no sustenance, but only an implacable slot of close air, a pocket within the earth. There is only one way you can live, now. There must be an anger to slap you awake, to make you move. A desire, a want, a need. Then you quiver and rise to strike your head against satin-lined wood. Life calls you. You grow with it. You claw upward, slowly, and find ways to displace the heavy earth an inch at a time, and one night you crumble the darkness, the exit is complete, and you burst forth to see the stars.

Now you stand, letting the emotion burn you. You take a step, like a child, stagger, clutch for support – and find a cold marble slab. Beneath your fingers the carved story of your life is briefly told: BORN – DIED.

You are a stick of wood, trying to walk. You go outward from the land of monuments, into twilight streets, alone on the pale sidewalks.

You feel something is left undone. Some flower yet unseen, some place you must see, some lake waiting for you to swim, some wine unsipped. You are going somewhere, to finish whatever is still undone.

The streets are strange. You walk through a town you have never seen, a dream on the rim of a lake. You grow more certain of your walking, you start to go quite swiftly. Memory returns.

Now you know every lawn of this street, every place

where asphalt bubbled from cement cracks in the summer oven weather. You know where the horses were tethered, sweating in the green spring at these iron waterfonts so long ago it is a fading mist in your brain. This cross street, where a lamp hangs like a bright spider spinning light across darkness. You escape its web into sycamore shadows. You run your fingers along a picket fence. Here, as a child, you rushed by with a stick raising a machine-gun racket, laughing.

These houses, holding their people and memories. The lemon odor of old Mrs Hanlon who lived here, a lady with withered hands who gave you a withered lecture on trampling her petunias. Now she is completely withered like an ancient paper burned.

The street is quiet except for the sound of someone walking. You turn a corner and unexpectedly collide with a stranger.

You both stand back. For a moment, examining each other, you understand.

The stranger's eyes are deep-seated fires. He is tall, thin, and wears a dark suit. There is a fiery whiteness in his cheekbones. He smiles. 'You're new,' he says.

You know then what he is. He is walking and 'different,' like you.

'Where are you going in such a hurry?' he asks.

'Step aside,' you say. 'I have no time. I have to go *somewhere*.'

He reaches out and grasps your elbow firmly. 'Do you

know *what* I am?' He bends close. 'Do you not realize
we are the same? We are as brothers.'

'I – I have no time.'

'No,' he agrees. 'Nor have I, to waste.'

You try to brush past, but he walks with you. 'I know
where you're going.'

'Yes?'

'Yes,' he says. 'To some childhood place. Some river.
Some house. Some memory. Some woman, perhaps. To
some old friend's bed. Oh, I know, I know everything
about our kind. I know.' He nods at the passing light
and dark.

'Do you?'

'That is always why we lost ones walk. Strange, when
you consider all the books written about ghosts and rest-
less souls – never once did the authors of those worthy
volumes touch upon the true secret of why we walk.
But it's always for a memory, a friend, a woman, a house,
a drink of wine, everything and anything connected to
life and . . . *living*!' He makes a fist to hold the words
tight. 'Living! *Real* living!'

Wordless, you increase your stride, but his whisper
follows:

'You must join me later, friend. We will meet with
the others, tonight, tomorrow, and all the nights until
at last, we win!'

'Who are the others?'

'The dead. We join against' – a pause – 'intolerance.'

'Intolerance?'

'We – the recently deceased, the newly interred – are a minority, a persecuted minority. *They* make laws against us!'

You stop walking. 'Minority?'

'Yes.' He grasps your arm. 'Are we wanted? No! We are feared, driven like sheep into a quarry, screamed at, stoned, like the Jews. It's wrong, I tell you, unfair!' He lifts his hands in fury and strikes the empty air. 'Is it fair that we melt in our graves while the rest of the world sings, laughs, dances? Fair, is it fair, that they love while we lie cold, that they touch while our hands turn to stone? No! I say down with them, down! Why should we die? Why not the others?'

'Maybe . . .'

'They slam the earth in our faces and carve a stone to weigh us down. They bring flowers and leave them to rot, once a year – sometimes not even that! Oh, how I hate the living. The damn fools! Dancing all night and loving till dawn, while we are abandoned. Is that right?'

'I hadn't thought of it that way . . .'

'Well,' he cries, 'we'll fix them.'

'How?'

'There are thousands of us gathering tonight in the Elysian grove. I will lead our army. We will march! They have neglected us for too long. If we can't live, then they won't! Will you come, friend? I have spoken with many. Join us. Tonight the graveyards will open and the lost ones will pour forth to drown the unbelievers. You will come?'

'Yes. Perhaps. But right now I must go. I am looking for something . . . Later, later I will join you.'

'Good,' he says. You walk off, leaving him in shadow. 'Good, good, good!'

Up the hill now, quickly. Thank God the night is cold.

You gasp. There, glowing in the night, but with simple magnificence, the house where Grandma sheltered and fed her boarders. Inside that grand, tall house, Saturday feasts happen. Where you as a child sat on the porch watching skyrockets climb in fire, the pinwheels sputtering, the gunpowder drumming at your ears from the brass cannon your uncle Bion fired with his hand-rolled cigarette.

Now, trembling with memory, you know why the dead walk. To see nights like this. Here, where dew littered the grass and you crushed the damp lawn, wrestling, and you knew the sweetness of now, now, tomorrow is gone, yesterday is done, tonight you live!

And here, here, remember? This is Kim's house. That yellow light around the back, that's her room.

You bang the gate wide and hurry up the walk.

You approach her window and feel your stale breath falling upon the cold glass. As the fog vanishes the shape of her room emerges: things spread on the little soft bed, the cherrywood floor brightly waxed, and throw-rugs like heavily furred dogs sleeping there.

She enters the room. She looks tired, but she sits and begins to comb her hair.

Breathlessly, you press your ear against the cold pane to listen, and as from a deep sea you hear her sing so softly it is already an echo before it is sung.

You tap on the windowpane.

But she doesn't turn; she continues combing her hair gently.

You tap again, anxiously.

This time she puts down the comb and rises to come to the window. At first she sees nothing; you are in shadow. Then she looks more closely. She sees a dim figure beyond the light.

'Kim!' You cannot help yourself. 'It's me! Kim!'

You push your face forward into the light. Her face pales. She does not cry out; but her eyes widen and her mouth opens as if a terrific lightning bolt has hit the earth beneath her. She pulls back slightly.

'Kim!' you cry. 'Kim.'

She says your name, but you can't hear it. She wants to run but instead she opens the window and, sobbing, stands back as you climb up and into the light.

You close the window and stand, swaying there, only to find her far across the room, her face half turned away.

You try to think of something to say, but cannot, and then you hear her crying.

At last she is able to speak.

'Six months,' she says. 'You've been gone that long. When you went away I cried. I never cried so much in my life. But now you *can't* be here.'

'I am!'

'But why? I don't understand,' she says. 'Why did you come?'

'I was lost. It was very dark and I started to dream; I don't know how. And there you were in the dream and I don't know how, but I had to find my way back.'

'You can't stay.'

'Until sunrise I can. I still love you.'

'Don't say that. You mustn't, anymore. I belong here and you belong there, and right now I'm terribly afraid. It's been so long. The things we did, the things we joked and laughed about, those things I still love, but—'

'I still think those thoughts. I think them over and over, Kim. Please try to understand.'

'You don't want pity, do you?'

'Pity?' You half turn away. 'No, I don't want that. Kim, listen to me. I could come visit you every night, we could talk just like we used to. I can explain, make you understand, if only you'll let me.'

'It's no use,' she says. 'We can never go back.'

'Kim, one hour every evening, or half an hour, anytime you say. Five minutes. Just to see you. That's all, that's all I ask.'

You try to take her hands. She pulls away.

She closes her eyes tightly and says simply, 'I'm afraid.'

'Why?'

'I've been taught to be afraid.'

'Is that it?'

'Yes, I guess that's it.'

'But I want to talk.'

'Talking won't help.'

Her trembling gradually passes and she becomes more calm and relaxed. She sinks down on the edge of the bed and her voice is very old in a young throat.

'Perhaps . . .' A pause. 'Maybe. I suppose a few minutes each night and maybe I'd get used to you and maybe I wouldn't be afraid.'

'Anything you say. You won't be afraid?'

'I'll try not to be.' She takes a deep breath. 'I won't be afraid. I'll meet you outside the house in a few minutes. Let me get myself together and we can say good night.'

'Kim, there's only one thing to remember: I love you.'

You climb back out the window and she pulls down the sash.

Standing there in the dark, you weep with something deeper than sorrow.

Across the street a man walks alone and you recognize him as the one who spoke to you earlier that night. He is lost and walking like you, alone in a world that he hardly knows.

And suddenly Kim is beside you.

'It's all right,' she says. 'I'm better now. I don't think I'm afraid.'

And together you stroll in the moonlight, just as you have so many times before. She turns you in at an ice-cream parlor and you sit at the counter and order ice cream.

You look down at the sundae and think how wonderful, it's been so long.

You pick up your spoon and put some of the ice cream in your mouth and then pause and feel the light in your face go out. You sit back.

'Something wrong?' the soda clerk behind the fountain says.

'Nothing.'

'Ice cream taste funny?'

'No, it's fine.'

'You ain't eating,' he says.

'No.'

You push the ice cream away and feel a terrible loneliness steal over you.

'I'm not hungry.'

You sit up very straight, staring at nothing. How can you tell her that you can't swallow, can't eat? How can you explain that your whole body seems to be solid, like a block of wood, and that nothing moves, nothing can be tasted?

Pushing back from the counter, you rise and wait for Kim to pay for the sundaes, and then you swing wide the door and walk out into the night.

'Kim—'

'It's all right,' she says.

You walk down toward the park. You feel her hand on your arm, a long way off, but the feeling is so soft that it is hardly there. Beneath your feet the sidewalk loses its solidity. You move without shock or bump, as if you're in a dream.

Kim says, 'Isn't that great? Smell the lilacs.'

You sniff the air but there is nothing. Panicked, you try again, but no lilac.

Two people pass in the dark. They drift by, smiling to Kim. As they move away one of them says, fading, 'Smell that? Something's rotten in Denmark.'

'What?'

'I don't see—'

'No!' Kim cries. And suddenly, at the sound of those voices, she starts to run.

You catch her arm. Silently you struggle. She beats at you. You can hardly feel her fists.

'Kim!' you cry. 'Don't. Don't be afraid.'

'Let go!' she cries. 'Let go.'

'I can't.'

Again the word: 'Can't.' She weakens and hangs, lightly sobbing against you. At your touch she trembles.

You hold her close, shivering. 'Kim, don't leave me. I have such plans. We'll travel, anywhere, just travel. Listen to me. Think of it. To eat the best food, to see the best places, to drink the best wine.'

Kim interrupts. You see her mouth move. You tilt your head. 'What?'

She speaks again. 'Louder,' you say. 'I can't hear you.'

She speaks, her mouth moves, but you hear absolutely nothing.

And then, as if from behind a wall, a voice says, 'It's no use. You see?'

You let her go.

'I wanted to see the light, flowers, trees, anything. I wanted to be able to touch you but, oh God, first, there, with the ice cream I tasted, it was all gone. And now I feel like I can't move. I can hardly hear your voice, Kim. A wind passed by in the night, but I hardly feel it.'

'Listen,' she says. 'This isn't the way. It takes more than wanting things to have them. If we can't talk or hear or feel or even taste, what is left for you or for me?'

'I can still see you and I remember the way we were.'

'That's not enough, there's got to be more than that.'

'It's unfair. God, I want to live!'

'You will, I promise that, but not like this.'

You stop. You turn very cold. Holding to her wrist, you stare into her moving face.

'What do you mean?'

'Our child. I'm carrying *our* child. You see, you didn't have to come back, you're always with me, you'll always be alive. Now turn around and go back. Believe me, everything will work out. Let me have a better memory than this terrible night with you. Go back where you came from.'

At this you cannot even weep; your eyes are dry. You hold her wrists tightly and then suddenly, without a word, she sinks slowly to the ground.

You hear her whisper, 'The hospital. Quick.'

You carry her down the street. A fog fills your left eye and you realize that soon you will be blind.

'Hurry,' she whispers. 'Hurry.'

You begin to run, stumbling.

A car passes and you flag it down. Moments later you and Kim are in the car with a stranger, roaring silently through the night.

And in the wild traveling you hear her repeat that she believes in the future and that you must leave soon.

At last you arrive and Kim has gone; the hospital attendant rushed her away without a good-bye.

You stand there, helpless, then turn and try to walk away. The world blurs.

Then you walk, finally, in half darkness, trying to see people, trying to smell any lilacs that still might be out there.

You find yourself entering the ravine just outside the park. The walkers are down there, the night walkers that gather. Remember what that man said? All those lost ones, all those lonely ones are coming together tonight to destroy those who do not understand them.

You stumble on the ravine path, fall, pick yourself up, and fall again.

The stranger, the walker, stands before you as you make your way toward the silent creek. You look around and there is no one else anywhere in the dark.

The strange leader cries out angrily, 'They did not come! Not one of those walkers, not one! Only you. Oh, the cowards, damn them, the damn cowards!'

'Good.' Your breath, or the illusion of breath, slows. 'I'm glad they didn't listen. There must be some reason. Perhaps – perhaps something happened to them that we can't understand.'

The leader shakes his head. 'I had plans. But I am alone. Yet even if all the lonely ones should rise, they are not strong. One blow and they fall. We grow tired. *I* am tired . . .'

You leave him behind. His whispers die. A dull pulse beats in your head. You leave the ravine and return to the graveyard.

Your name is on the gravestone. The raw earth awaits you. You slide down the narrow tunnel into satin and wood, no longer afraid or excited. You lie suspended in warm darkness. You relax.

You are overwhelmed by a luxury of warm sustenance, like a great yeast; you feel as if you are buoyed by a whispering tide.

You breathe quietly, not hungry, not worried. You are

deeply loved. You are secure. This place where you lie dreaming shifts, moves.

Drowsy. Your body is melting, it is small, compact, weightless. Drowsy. Slow. Quiet. Quiet.

Who are you trying to remember? A name moves out to sea. You run to fetch it, the waves bear it away. Someone beautiful. Someone. A time, a place. Sleepy. Darkness, warmth. Soundless earth. Dim tide. Quiet.

A dark river bears you faster and yet faster.

You break into the open. You are suspended in hot yellow light.

The world is immense as a snow mountain. The sun blazes and a huge red hand seizes your feet as another hand strikes your back to force a cry from you.

A woman lies near. Sweat beads her face, and there is a wild singing and a sharp wonder to this room and this world. You cry out, upside down, and are swung right side up, cuddled and nursed.

In your small hunger, you forget talking, you forget all things. Her voice, above, whispers:

'Dear baby. I will name you for him. For . . . him . . .'

These words are nothing. Once you feared something terrifying and black, but now it is forgotten in this warmth. A name forms in your mouth, you try to say it, not knowing what it means, only able to cry it happily. The word vanishes, fades, an erased ghost of laughter in your head.

'Kim! Kim! Oh, *Kim*!'

Remembrance, Ohio

They came running through the hot still dust of town, with their shadows burned black under them by the sun.

They held on to picket fences. They clutched trees. They seized lilac bushes, which gave no support, so they swayed and grabbed at each other, then ran on and looked back. With abrupt focus, the empty street rushed at them. They gasped and wheeled in a clumsy dance.

And then they saw it and made sounds like travelers at noon finding a landfall mirage, an incredible isle promising cool breezeways and water glades melted out of forgotten snows.

Ahead stood a cream-white house with a grape-arbor porch hummed about by bees with golden pelts.

'Home,' said the woman. 'We'll be safe there!'

The man blinked at the house in surprise. 'I don't understand . . .'

But they helped each other up onto the porch and sat precisely down in the swing, which hung like a special scale weighing them, and them afraid of the total.

The only movement for a long time now was the drift of the swing going nowhere with two people perched precariously, birdlike, in it. The street laid out its hot roll of dust on which no footprints or tire marks were stenciled. On occasion a wind paraded from nowhere, down the center of the dusty road to lie down under cool green trees. Beyond that, everything was baked solid. If you ran up on any porch and spat on any window and rubbed the grime away, you might peek in to find the dead, like so many clay mummies, scattered on the carpetless floors. But nobody ran, spat, or looked.

'Shh,' she whispered.

There were hummingbird flickers of leafy sunlight on their still faces.

'You *hear*?'

Somewhere far off, a drift of voices slid away. A siren bubbled, rose, then stopped. The dust settled. The noises of the world drifted lazily to rest.

The woman glanced over at her husband on the seat beside her.

'Will they find us? We did escape, we *are* free, *aren't* we?'

He barely nodded. He was about thirty-five, a man all

bristly and pink. The pink veins in his eyes made the rest of him seem infinitely redder, warmer, more irritable. He often told her he had this great hair ball in him, which made it hard to speak, much less breathe, in hot weather. Panic was a continual way of life for both of them. If one drop of rain fell on his hand from the blind sky now, it might jolt him into rabbiting off and leaving her alone.

She moved her tongue on her lips.

The small motion fretted him. Her coolness was a bother.

She took a chance on speaking again. 'It's nice to sit.'

His nod made the porch swing glide.

'Mrs Haydecker'll be coming up the street with a whole crate of fresh-picked strawberries any moment,' she said.

He frowned.

'Right out of her garden,' she added.

The grapevines grew quietly over the cool dark porch. They felt like children hiding out from parents.

Sunlight picked the tiny silver hairs on a geranium stalk potted on the railing. It made the man feel like he was trapped in his winter underwear.

She arose suddenly and went to peer at the doorbell button and reached out as if to touch it.

'Don't!' he said.

Too late; she had planted her thumb on the button.

'It's not working.' She slapped her hand over her mouth and talked through the fingers. 'Silly! Ringing your own doorbell. To see if I came to the door and looked out at myself?'

'Get away from there.' He was on his feet now. 'You'll spoil everything!'

But she could not keep her child's hand from prowling to twist the doorknob.

'Unlocked! Why, it was always locked!'

'Hands off!'

'I won't try to go in.' Suddenly she reached up to run her fingertips along the top of the sill. 'Someone stole the key, that explains it. Stole it and went in and I bet robbed the house. We stayed away too long.'

'We only been gone an hour.'

'Don't lie,' she said. 'You know it's been months. No . . . what? Years.'

'An hour,' he said. 'Sit down.'

'It was such a long trip. I think I will.' But she still held on to the doorknob. 'I want to be fresh when I yell at Mama, "Mama, we're here!" I wonder where Benjamin is? Such a good dog.'

'Dead,' said the man, forgetting. 'Ten years ago.'

'Oh . . .' She backed off and her voice softened. 'Yes . . .' She eyed the door, the porch, and beyond, the town. 'Something's wrong. I can't name it. But something's wrong!'

The only sound was the sun burning the sky.

'Is this California or Ohio?' she said, at last turning to him.

'Don't *do* that!' He seized her wrist. 'This is California.'

'What's our town doing here?' she demanded, wildly out of breath. 'When it used to be in Ohio!'

'We're lucky we found this! Don't talk about it!'

'Or maybe this *is* Ohio. Maybe we never went west, years ago.'

'This,' he said, 'is California.'

'What's the name of this place?'

'Coldwater.'

'You *sure*?'

'On a hot day like *this*? Coldwater.'

'You sure this isn't Mellow Glen? Or Breezeway Falls?'

'At high noon, those all sound good.'

'Maybe it's Inclement, Nebraska.' She smiled. 'Or Devil's Prong, Idaho. Or Boiling Sands, Montana.'

'Go back to the icehouse names,' he said.

'Mint Willow, Illinois.'

'Ahh.' He closed his eyes.

'Snow Mountain, Missouri.'

'Yes.' He stirred the swing and they swung back and forth.

'But I know the best,' she said. 'Remembrance. That's where we are. Remembrance, Ohio.'

And by his smiling silence, eyes shut as they glided, she knew that indeed was were they were.

'Will *they* find us here?' she asked, suddenly apprehensive.

'Not if we're careful, not if we hide.'

'Oh!' she said.

Because at the far end of the street, in the glare of bright sun, a group of men appeared suddenly, fanning out in the dust.

'There they are! Oh, what've we done that they chase us this way? Are we robbers, Tom, or thieves, did we kill someone?'

'No, but they followed us here to Ohio, anyway.'

'I thought you said this was California.'

He lolled his head back and stared into the blazing sky. 'God, I don't know anymore. Maybe they put the town on rollers.'

The strangers, a short way off in their own world of dust, were pausing now. You could hear their voices barking under the trees.

'We've got to run, Tom! Let's move!' She tugged at his elbow, tried to pull him to his feet.

'Yeah, but look. All the little things that're wrong. The town . . .' He glided, loose-mouthed, loose-eyed, in the swing. 'This house. Something about the porch. Used to be three steps coming up. Now it's four.'

'No!'

'I felt the change, with my feet. And those stained-glass panes around the door window, they're blue and red. Used to be orange and milk white.'

He gestured with a tired hand.

'And the sidewalks, trees, houses. Whole damn town. I can't *figure* it.'

She stared and it began to come clear what it was. Someone with a big hand had scooped up the entire known familiar town of her childhood – the churches, garages, windows, porches, attics, bushes, lawns, lamp-posts – and poured it into a glass oven, there to know a fever so intense that everything melted and warped. Houses expanded a little too large or shrunk too small from their old size, sidewalks tilted, steeples grew. Whoever had glued the town back together had lost the blueprint. It was beautiful but strange.

'Yes,' she murmured. 'Yes, you're right. I used to know every crack in the sidewalk with my roller skates. It's *not* the same.'

The strangers came running and turned off at an alley.

'They're going around the block,' she said. 'Then they'll find us here.'

'I don't know,' he said. 'Maybe, maybe not.'

They sat, not moving, listening to the hot green silence.

'I know what I want,' she said. 'I want to go in the house and open the icebox door and drink some cold milk and go in the pantry and smell the bananas hung on a string from the ceiling, and eat a powdered doughnut out of the bin.'

'Don't try to go into the house,' he said, eyes shut. 'You'll be sorry.'

She leaned over to look into his drawn face.

'You're scared.'

'Me?'

'To do a simple thing like open the front door!'

'Yes,' he said, finally. 'I'm scared. We can't run any further. They'll catch us and take us back to that place.'

She laughed suddenly. 'Weren't they funny people? Wouldn't take money from us for staying there. I liked the women's costumes, all white and starched.'

'I didn't like the windows,' he said. 'The metal grating. Remember when I made a noise like a hacksaw and the men came running?'

'Yes. Why do they always run?'

'Because we know too much, that's why.'

'I don't know anything,' she said.

'They hate you for being you and me for being me.'

They heard voices in the distance.

The woman took a mirror from a wadded handkerchief in her pocket, breathed on it, and smiled in welcome. 'I'm alive. Sometimes, in that place, I lay on the floor and said I was dead and they couldn't bother me anymore. But they threw water on me and made me stand up.'

Shouting, six men turned the corner fifty yards away and started toward the house where the man and woman sat in the swing, fanning their faces with their hands.

'What did we do to be hunted like this?' said the woman. 'Will they kill us?'

'No, they'll talk soft and kind and walk us back out of town.'

He jumped up, suddenly.

'Now what?' she cried.

'I'm going inside and wake your mother from her nap,' he said. 'And we'll sit at the round table in the living room and have peach shortcake with whipped cream, and when those men knock on the door, your mother'll just tell them to go away. We'll eat with the silverware your mother got from the *Chicago Tribune* in 1928 with those pictures of Thomas Meighan and Mary Pickford on the handles.'

She smiled. 'We'll play the phonograph. We'll play the record "The Three Trees, There, There, and – There!"'

'Come on,' he said. 'We have to go!'

The six men spied the man and woman on the dim front porch, shouted, and ran forward.

'Hurry!' screamed the woman. 'Get inside, call Mother and Sister, oh, hurry, here they *come*!'

He flung the front door wide.

She rushed in after him, slammed the door, and turned.

There was nothing behind the front wall of the house except strutworks, canvas, boards, a small meadow, and a creek. A few arc-lights stood to each side. Stenciled on one papier-mâché inner wall was STUDIO #12.

Footsteps thundered on the front porch.

The door banged open. The men piled in.

'Oh!' the woman screamed. 'The *least* you could do is *knock*!'

If Paths Must Cross Again

It was almost unbelievable when they found out. Dave Lacey couldn't believe it, and Theda didn't dare. It shocked them gently, stunned them, then turned them a bit cold, and they were sad and wondrous all at once.

'No, it can't be,' insisted Theda, clenching his hand. 'It just can't. I went to Central School, the eighth grade, and that was in 1933, and you—'

'Sure,' said Dave, delightedly out of breath. 'I came to town in 1933, right there to Brentwood, Illinois, I swear it, and I roomed in the YMCA right across the street from Central School for six months. My parents had divorce troubles in Chicago and packed me off up there from April to September!'

'Oh, Lord.' She sighed. 'What floor did you live on?'

'The fifth,' said he. He lit a cigarette, gave it to her,

lit another, and leaned back against the leather wall of the La Bomba cocktail lounge. Soft music played somewhere in dimness; both paid it no heed. He snapped his fingers. 'I used to eat at Mick's, half a block down the street from the Y.'

'Mick's!' cried Theda. 'I ate there, too. Mother said it was a horrid greasy sort of place, so I ate there on the sly. Oh, Lordy, David, all those years ago, and we didn't even know it!'

His eyes were distant, thinking back quietly. He nodded gently. 'Why, I ate at Mick's every noon. Sat down at the end where I could watch girls from school walk by in bright dresses.'

'And here we are in Los Angeles, two thousand miles away and ten years removed from it, and I'm twenty-four,' said Theda, 'and you're twenty-nine, and it took us all these years to meet!'

He shook his head uncomprehendingly. 'Why didn't I find you then?'

'Maybe we weren't supposed to meet then.'

'Maybe,' he said, 'I was scared. That's probably it. I was a frightened sort. Girls had to waylay me. I wore horn-rims and carried thick books under my arm instead of muscles. Lord, Lord, Theda, darling, I ate more hamburgers at Mike's.'

'With big hunks of onion,' said Theda. 'And hotcakes with syrup. Remember?' She began to think and it was hard, looking at him. 'I don't remember you, Dave.

I send my mind back, searching frantically, back a decade, and I never saw you then. At least not the way you are now.'

'Perhaps you snubbed me.'

'I did if you flirted.'

'No. I only remember looking at a blond girl.'

'A blond girl in Brentwood in the year 1933,' said Theda. 'In Mike's at twelve o'clock on a spring day.' Theda thought back. 'How was she dressed?'

'All I remember is a blue ribbon in her hair, tied in a large bow, and I have an impression of a blue polka-dot dress and young breasts just beginning to rise. Oh, she was pretty.'

'Do you remember her face, Dave?'

'Only that she was beautiful. You don't remember single faces out of a crowd after so much time's passed. Think of all the people you meet on the street every day, Theda.'

She closed her eyes. 'If I'd only known then that I'd meet you later in life, I would have looked for you.'

He laughed ironically. 'But you never know those things. You see too many people every week, every year, and most of them are destined for obscurity. All you can do, later, is look back at the dim movements of the years and see where your life briefly touched, flickered against another's. The same town, the same restaurant, the same food, the same air, but two different paths and ways of living, oblivious one of the other.' He kissed her fingers.

'I should have kept my eyes open for you, too. But the only girl I noticed was that blond girl with the ribbon hair.'

It irritated her. 'We rubbed elbows, we actually passed on the street. Why, on summer nights, I bet you were down at the carnival at the lake.'

'Yes, I went down. I looked at the colored lights reflected in the water and heard the merry-go-round music jangling at the stars!'

'I remember, I remember,' she said eagerly. 'And maybe some nights you went to the Academy Theatre?'

'I saw Harold Lloyd's picture *Welcome Danger* there that summer.'

'Yes, yes. I was there. I remember. And they had a short feature with Ruth Etting singing "Shine On, Harvest Moon." Follow the bouncing ball.'

'You've got a memory,' he said.

'Darling, so near and yet so far. Do you realize we practically knocked each other down going by for six months. It's murderous! Those brief months together and then ten years until this year. It happens all the time. We live a block from people in New York, never see them, go to Milwaukee and meet them at a party. And tomorrow night—'

She stopped talking. Her face paled and she held his strong tanned fingers. Dim lights played off his lieutenant's bars, winking them strangely, hypnotically.

He had to finish it for her, slowly. 'Tomorrow night I

go away again. Overseas. So damn soon, oh, so damn soon.' He made a fist and beat the table slowly, with no noise. After a while he looked at his wristwatch and exhaled. 'We'd better go, darling. It's late.'

'No,' she said. 'Please, Dave, just a moment more.' She looked at him. 'I've got the awfulest feeling. I'm scared stiff. I'm sorry.'

He closed his eyes, opened them, looked around, and saw the faces. Theda did likewise. Perhaps they both thought the same strange thoughts.

'Look around, Theda,' he said. 'Remember all these faces. Maybe, if I don't come back, you may meet someone else again and you'll go with them six months and suddenly discover that your paths crossed before – on a July night 1944 at a cocktail place called La Bomba on the Sunset Strip. And, oh yeah, you were with a young lieutenant named David Lacey that night, whatever happened to him? Oh, he went to war and didn't come back – and well, by gosh, you'll discover that one of these faces in the room right now was here seeing this, seeing me talk to you now, noting your beauty and hearing me say "I love you, I love you." Remember these faces, Theda, and maybe they'll remember us, and—'

Her fingers went upon his lips, sealing in any other words. She was crying and afraid and her eyes blinked a wet film through which she saw the many faces of people looking her way, and she thought of all the paths and patterns, and it was awful, the future, David—

She looked at him again, holding him so tightly, and she said that she loved him over and over.

And all the rest of the evening he was a boy in horn-rims with books under his arm, and she was a golden-haired girl with a very blue ribbon tied in her long bright hair . . .

Miss Appletree and I

No one remembered how it began with Miss Appletree. It seemed Miss Appletree had been around for years. Every time Nora made a bad biscuit or didn't put on her lipstick when she came to the breakfast table, George would laughingly say, 'Watch out! I'll run off with Miss Appletree!'

Or when George had his night out with the boys and came home slightly eroded and worn away by the sands of time, Nora would say, 'Well, how was Miss Appletree?'

'Fine, fine,' George would say. 'But I love only you, Nora. It's good to be home.'

As you can see, Miss Appletree was around the house for years, invisible as the smell of grass in April, or the scent of chestnut leaves falling in October.

George even described her: 'She's tall.'

'I'm five feet seven in my stocking feet,' said Nora.

'She's willowy,' said George.

'I'm spreading a bit with the years,' said Nora.

'And she's fairy yellow in the hair.'

'My hair is turning mousy,' said Nora. 'It used to shine like the sun.'

'She's a quiet sort,' said George.

'I gossip far too much,' said Nora.

'And she loves me blindly, passionately, with not a doubt in her mind or soul, wildly, insanely,' said George, 'as no woman with brains could ever love a shameful bumbling old drone like me.'

'She sounds like an avalanche,' said Nora.

'But do you know,' said George, 'when the avalanche rolls away and life must go on, I always turn to you, Nora. Miss Appletree is quite impossible. I always come back to my one and only love, the woman who doubts I am a God after all, the woman who knows I put my right foot into my left shoe and is diplomatic enough to give me two right shoes at a time like that, the woman who realizes that I'm a weather vane in every wind yet never tries to tell me that the sun rises in the east and sets in the west, so why am I lost? Nora, you know every pore in my face, every hair in my ear, every cavity in my teeth; but I love you.'

'Fare thee well, Miss Appletree!' said Nora.

And so the years went by.

'Hand me the hammer and some nails,' said George one day.

'Why?' said his wife.

'This calendar,' he said. 'I'm going to nail it down. The leaves fall off it like a deck of cards somebody dropped. Good Lord, I'm fifty years old today! Hand me that hammer quick!'

She came and kissed his cheek. 'You don't mind terribly, do you?'

'I didn't mind yesterday,' he said. 'But today I mind. What is there about units of ten that so frightens a man? When a man's twenty-nine years old and nine months it doesn't faze him. But on his thirtieth birthday, O Fates and Furies, life is over, love is done and dead, the career is up the flue or down the chute, either way. And a man goes along the next ten, twenty years, through thirty, past forty, on toward fifty, reasonably keeping his hands off Time, not trying to hold on to the days too hard, letting the wind blow and the river run. But Good Lord, all of a sudden you're fifty years old, that nice round total, that grand sum and – bang! Depression and horror. Where *have* the years gone? What *has* one done with one's life?'

'One has raised a daughter and a son, both married young and gone already,' said Nora. 'And proud children they are!'

'True,' said George. 'And yet on a day like this, in the middle of May, it feels sad, like autumn. You know me,

I'm a moody old dog. I'm the son of Thomas Wolfe, O Time, O River, oh, the grieving of the winds, lost, lost, forever lost.'

'You need Miss Appletree,' said Nora.

He blinked. 'I need what?'

'Miss Appletree,' said Nora. 'The lady we made up such a long time ago. Tall, willowy, madly in love with you. Miss Appletree, the magnificent. Aphrodite's daughter. Every man turned fifty, every man who's feeling sorry for himself and feeling sad needs Miss Appletree. Romance.'

'Oh, but I have you, Nora,' he said.

'Oh, but I'm neither as young nor as pretty as I once was,' Nora said, taking his arm. 'Once in his lifetime, every man should have his fling.'

'Do you really think so?' he said.

'I know it!'

'But that causes divorce. Foolish old men rushing about after their youth.'

'Not if the wife has a head on her shoulders. Not if she understands he's not being mean, he's just very sad and lost and tired and mixed up.'

'I know so many men who've run off with Miss Appletrees, alienated their wives and children, and made a mess of their lives.'

He brooded for a moment and then said, 'Well, I've been thinking a lot of hard thoughts every minute of every hour of every day. One shouldn't think of young women that much. That's not good and it might have some sort of force of nature and I don't think I should be thinking that way, so hard and so intense.'

He was finishing his breakfast when the front door-bell rang. He and Nora looked at each other and then there was a soft tapping at the door.

He looked as if he wanted to get up but couldn't force himself, so Nora rose and walked to the front door. She turned the knob slowly and looked out. A conversation followed.

He closed his eyes and listened and thought he heard two women talking out on the front stoop. One of the voices was soft and the other voice seemed to be gaining strength.

A few minutes later, Nora returned to the table.

'Who was that?' he said.

'A saleslady,' Nora said.

'A what?'

'A saleslady.'

'What was she selling?'

'She told me but she talked so quietly that I could hardly hear.'

'What was her name?'

'I couldn't quite catch it,' said Nora.

'What did she look like?'

'She was tall.'

'How tall?'

'Very tall.'

'And nice to look at?'

'Nice.'

'What color hair?'

'It was like sunlight.'

'So.'

'So,' Nora said. 'Now, I tell you what. Drink that coffee, stand up, go back upstairs, and get back into bed.'

'Say that again,' he said.

'Drink that coffee, stand up . . .' she said.

He stared at her, slowly picked up his coffee cup, drained it, and began to rise.

'But,' he said, 'I'm not sick. I don't need to go back to bed this early in the morning.'

'You look a little poorly,' said Nora. 'I'm giving you an order. Go upstairs, take off your clothes, and go to bed.'

He turned slowly and walked up the stairs and felt himself taking off his clothes and lying down in the bed. As soon as his head hit the pillow, he had to fight not to fall asleep.

A few moments later he heard a stirring in the somewhat dim early-morning room.

He felt someone lie down in the bed and turn toward him. Eyes shut, he heard his voice groggily ask, 'What? Who's there?'

A voice murmured to him from the next pillow. 'Miss Appletree.'

'How's that again?' he said.

'Miss Appletree' was the whisper.

A Literary Encounter

It had been going on for a long time, but perhaps she first gave it notice this autumn evening when Charlie was walking the dog and met her on the way back from the grocer's. They had been married a year, but it wasn't often they happened on each other this way, like two strangers.

'God, it's good to see you, Marie!' he cried, taking her arm fiercely. His dark eyes were shining and he was sniffing great lungfuls of the sharp air. 'God, isn't it a lost evening, though!'

'It's nice.' She looked quietly at him as they walked toward their house.

'October,' he gasped. 'Lord, I love to be out in it, eating it, breathing it, smelling its smell. Oh, it's a wild, sad month, all right. Look at the way the trees are burning with it. The world's on fire in October; and you think of all the dead you'll never see again.' He gripped her hand tightly.

'Just a minute. The dog wants to stop.'

They waited in the cold darkness while the dog tapped a tree with his nose.

'God, smell that incense!' The husband stretched. 'I feel tall tonight, like I could stride the earth, yank down stars, start volcanoes roaring!'

'Is your headache gone from this morning?' she asked softly.

'Gone, Christ, it'll *never* come back! Who thinks of headaches on such a night! Listen to the leaves rustle! Listen to that wind in the high and empty trees! God, isn't it a lonely, lost time, though, and where are we going, we lost and wandering souls on the brick pavements of the surging cities and little lonely towns where the trains pound through the night? I'd love to be traveling tonight, oh, traveling anywhere, to be out in it, drinking its wildness, its sad sweetness!'

'Why don't we ride the trolley out to Chessman Park tonight, it's a nice ride,' she said, nodding.

He flung up a hand, urging on the slow dog. 'No, I mean *really* traveling! Over bridges and hills and by cold cemeteries and past hidden villages where lights are all out and nobody knows you're passing in the night on ringing steel!'

'Well, then, we might take the North Shore up to Chicago for the weekend,' she suggested.

He looked at her pitiably in the dark and crushed her small cool hand in his mighty one. 'No,' he said with grand simplicity. 'No.' He turned. 'Come on. Home to a huge dinner. Three steaks, I want, a glutton's repast! Rare red wines, rich sauces, and a steaming tureen of creamed soup, with an after-dinner liqueur, and—'

'We've pork chops and peas.' She unlocked the front door.

On the way to the kitchen, she tossed her hat. It landed on an opened copy of Thomas Wolfe's *Of Time and the River,* which lay under the hurricane lamp. Giving her husband a look, she ran to investigate the potatoes.

Three nights passed in which he stirred violently in bed when the wind blew. He stared with intent brightness at the window rattling in the autumn storm. Then, he relaxed.

The following evening, when she entered from snatching a few sheets off the line, she found him seated deep in his library chair, a cigarette hanging from his lower lip.

'Drink?' he said.

'Yes,' she said.

'What?'

'What do you mean, "what?"' she asked.

A faint tinge of irritation moved in his impassive cold face.

'What *kind*?' he said.

'Scotch,' she said.

'Soda?' he said.

'Right.' She felt her face take on the same expression-less aspect as his.

He lunged over to the cabinet, took out a couple glasses big as vases, and perfunctorily filled them.

'Okay?' He gave her hers.

She looked at it. 'Fine.'

'Dinner?' He eyed her coldly, over his drink.

'Steak.'

'Hash browns?' His lips were a thin line.

'Right.'

'Good girl.' He laughed a little, bleakly, tossing the drink into his hard mouth, eyes closed.

She lifted her drink. 'Luck.'

'You said it.' He thought it over slyly, eyes moving about the room. 'Another?'

'Don't mind,' she said.

'Atta girl,' he said. 'Atta baby.'

He shot soda into her glass. It sounded like a fire hose let loose in the silence. He walked back to lose himself like a little boy in the immense library chair. Just before sinking behind a copy of Dashiell Hammett's *The Maltese Falcon*, he drawled, 'Call me.'

She turned her glass slowly in her hand that was like a white tarantula.

'Check,' she said.

*   *   *

She watched him for another week. She found herself frowning most of the time. Several times she felt like screaming.

As she watched, one evening, he seated himself at dinner and said:

'Madame, you look absolutely exquisite tonight.'

'Thank you.' She passed the corn.

'A most extraordinary circumstance occurred at the office today,' he said. 'A gentleman called to ascertain my health. "Sir," I said politely. "I am in excellent equilibrium, and am in no need of your services." "Oh, but, sir," he said, "I am representative of such-and-so's insurance company, and I wish only to give into your hands this splendid and absolutely irreproachable policy." Well, we conversed pleasantly enough, and, resultantly, this evening, I am the proud possessor of a new life insurance, double indemnity and all, which protects you under all circumstances, dear kind lady love of my life.'

'How nice,' she said.

'Perhaps you will also be pleased to learn,' he said, 'that for the last few days, beginning on the night of Thursday last, I became acquainted and charmed with the intelligent and certain prose of one Samuel Johnson. I am now amidst his *Life of Alexander Pope*.'

'So much I assumed,' she said, 'from your demeanor.'

'Eh?' He held his knife and fork politely before him.

'Charlie,' she said wistfully. 'Could you do me a big favor?'

'Anything.'

'Charlie, do you remember when we married a year ago?'

'But yes; every sweet, singular instant of our courtship!'

'Well, Charlie, do you remember what books you were reading during our courtship?'

'Is it of importance, my darling?'

'Very.'

He put himself to it with a scowl. 'I cannot remember,' he admitted finally. 'But I shall attempt to recall during the evening.'

'I wish you would,' she urged. 'Because, well, because I'd like you to start reading those books again, those books, whatever they were, which you read when first we met. You swept me from my feet with your demeanor then. But since, you've – changed.'

'Changed? *I?*' He drew back as from a cold draft.

'I wish you'd start reading those same books again,' she repeated.

'But why do you desire this?'

'Oh, because.'

'Truly a woman's reason.' He slapped his knees. 'But I shall try to please. As soon as I recall, I shall read those books once more.'

'And, Charlie, one more thing, promise to read them every day for the rest of your life?'

'Your wish, dear lady, my command. Please pass the salt.'

But he did not remember the names of the books.

The long evening passed and she looked at her hands, biting her lips.

Promptly at eight o'clock, she jumped up, crying out, 'I remember!'

In a matter of instants she was in their car, driving down the dark streets to town, into a bookstore where, laughing, she bought ten books.

'Thank you!' said the book dealer. 'Good night!'

The door slammed with a tinkle of bells.

Charlie read late at night, sometimes fumbling to bed, blind with literature, at three in the morning.

Now, at ten o'clock, before retiring, Marie slipped into the library, laid the ten books quietly next to Charlie, and tiptoed out.

She watched through the library keyhole, her heart beating loudly in her. She was in a perfect fever.

After a time, Charlie glanced up at the desk. He blinked at the new books. Hesitantly, he closed his copy of Samuel Johnson, and sat there.

'Go on,' whispered Marie through the keyhole. 'Go on!' Her breath came and went in her mouth.

Charlie licked his lips thoughtfully and then, slowly, he put out his hand. Taking one of the new books, he opened it, settled down, and began reading.

Singing softly, Marie walked off to bed.

He bounded into the kitchen the next morning with a glad cry. 'Hello, beautiful woman! Hello, lovely, wonderful, kind, understanding creature, living in this great wide sweet world!'

She looked at him happily. 'Saroyan?' she said.

'Saroyan!' he cried, and they had breakfast.

America

We are the dream that other people dream.
  The land where other people land.
  When late at night
  They think on flight
  And, flying, here arrive
  Where we fools dumbly thrive ourselves.
  Refuse to see
  We be what all the world would like to be.
  Because we hive within this scheme
  The obvious dream is blind to us.
  We do not mind the miracle we are,
  So stop our mouths with curses.
  While all the world rehearses
  Coming here to stay.
  We busily make plans to go away.

How dumb! newcomers cry, arrived from Chad.
You're mad! Iraqis shout.
We'd sell our souls if we could be you.
How come you cannot see the way we see you?
You tread a freedom forest as you please.
But, damn! You miss the forest for the trees.
Ten thousand wanderers a week
Engulf your shore,
You wonder what their shouting's for,
And why so glad?
Run warm those souls: America is bad?
Sit down, stare in their faces, see!
You be the hoped-for thing a hopeless world would be.
In tides of immigrants that this year flow
You still remain the beckoning hearth they'd know.
In midnight beds with blueprint, plan and scheme
You are the dream that other people dream.

Spares

Michael Marshall Smith

Spares – human clones, the ultimate in health insurance. An eye for an eye, but some people are doing all the taking.

Spares – the story of Jack Randall: burnt-out, dropped out, and with a zero credit rating at the luck bank. After five years lying low on a Spares Farm, looking after inmates that can't even spell luck, he is finally faced with a chance at redemption . . . if he, and the spares, can run fast enough.

Spares – it's fiction. But only just . . .

'Comic, cruel, twisted and surreal'
Empire

'Witty, hard-edged and coruscatingly imaginative . . . compellingly off-kilter'
New Scientist

'Smith masterfully moves the whodunit toward the future, opening up refreshing vistas for a genre rooted in the present'
People Magazine

ISBN: 0-00-651267-4

The Court of the Air
By Stephen Hunt

Two orphans on the run, each with the power to save the world . . .

When streetwise Molly Templar witnesses a brutal murder at the brothel she has recently been apprenticed to, her first instinct is to scurry back to the poorhouse where she grew up. But there she finds her fellow orphans butchered, and it slowly dawns on her that she was the real target of the attack.

Oliver Brooks has led a sheltered existence in the back-water home of his merchant uncle. But when he is framed for his only relative's murder he is forced to flee for his life, accompanied by an agent of the mysterious Court of the Air.

Molly and Oliver each carry secrets in their blood – secrets that will either get them killed or save the world from an ancient terror. Thrown into the company of outlaws, thieves and spies as they flee their ruthless enemies, the two orphans are also aided by indomitable friends in this endlessly inventive tale full of drama, intrigue and adventure.

'Convincing and colourful . . . compulsive reading'
Guardian

ISBN: 978-0-00-723218-5

£7.99